Islands in the Sky

Morgan's Knot – A Serial Fantasy

Episode V

By

Eric Thomas Stiller, Jr.

For our children's
children's children

Islands in the Sky

Morgan's Knot – A Serial Fantasy
Episode V

Far too addled to focus on his studies, Adrian closed his book of sonnets and set it aside, his concentration lost in a conflux of visions and memories tumbling and tangling through his mind. While awed by the wonder of the creatures populating the plane of the animals in perfect balance, he suffered the looming threat of Legio Obscurum's quest for domination of the real world in the very core of his being.

The true miracle of life on this planet and immanent terror, at the hands of an invisible army, were the stuff of fantasy to the rest of humanity. After exposing the secrets in New York, he wondered whether mankind would see the incident as some curious entertainment or a glimpse into the promise of our future?

Gazing around the room in utter distraction, he spied the pouch hanging on the back of the chair at his desk, untouched since the destruction of Zepallo's underground complex and the invasion of the United Nations. There was a bulge in the bag, the Black Book that he snagged from the floor of the Dark Lord's lair. It was smaller but, certainly, as heavy as the Book of Wisdoms. The metallic cover reflected the warm light, cast from the *orb* hovering above his headboard, as cold and dull.

"I should have given this to the Professor," he thought, fingering the Book and sensing the bristling static of dark energies. A surge, from somewhere deep inside his consciousness, raised prickly goosebumps on his skin and warned of danger. *"Raffe said this Book contains the history and the future of all of the Powers. I wonder whether it might give us a glimpse into the plans of Legio Obscurum?"*

Adrian's fingers tingled as he lifted the cover and stared at facing pages, swirling smoke under glass. The numbing chill, suffered when he first sensed the dark power radiating from the conical black mountain dominating the north end of the island or when Zepallo was close, raced up his spine to detonate at the base of his skull.

There were no familiar figures wandering about the pages, so he asked, "Where is Zepallo?"

The haze on the folio churned into roiling storm clouds, propelling little waves crashing against the edges to flow back across the Book in pulsing hypnotic ripples. Slowly, two colorless eyes emerged from the pages and a deep voice replied, "He is here, he is everywhere."

"Tell me about Legio Obscurum."

"A *seer* of our domain would have intimate knowledge of our history and affairs of state. The secrets the uninitiated might discover in this Book reach back to the dawn of evolution and forward to the end of times. Are you sure you want to know the answer to your question?"

"Tell me!"

"Long ago, there was a global battle between patrons of the Dark and the Light. Accepting the prospect of terminal stalemate after a thousand years of war, the Dark Forces withdrew to restore an underground civilization that has since expanded to dominate every country on the planet. Efforts to regain control of the political, religious, and economic powers required centuries of diligent patience, but the time is nearing when the Dark Forces will overwhelm the Light. Whisperers have been placed in positions of power and influence and it is only a matter of time before they will be freed to fulfill their directives."

"What countries will begin this conquest?"

Cold eyes stared for a long moment, "A better question might be which countries will not join in this revolution? There are very few not approaching total dominion from within by the emissaries of Legio Obscurum, under the direction of the Council of Ollapez."

Adrian stared at the pages, dumbfounded by the response, "How can this be?"

"Consider the major powers. Each of the industrialized nations is being transformed into a two-class society, comprised of those who rule and those who serve. Individual rights and liberties, the very foundation of Western civilization, are being withdrawn or abridged in the name of security with patriotic zeal. Radical elements from every religion in the world are leading their flocks toward oblivious compliance. Loud fanatical voices, claiming absolute devotion, have gained more attention than those who are truly devout. Cries of, 'Believe as I believe!' and 'Either you stand with us or you stand in our way!' echo in a hundred languages from all sides of every conflict or disagreement throughout the world. Scientific research is dwindling, as funding is managed and controlled by those who serve, and fluctuating markets are destroying any hope of financial security. The media is filled with stories containing subliminal messages, weaving a universal sense of fear into the public consciousness and slowly desensitizing the masses to the coming carnage and their subservience to the Dark Powers. There will be great battles but, in the end, every society in the world will turn to our leaders for salvation, because there will be no other viable alternative."

Adrian stared into the eyes in the Book. "Will those who defend the Powers of the Light prevail?"

"The evidence suggests complete capitulation."

Adrian realized that the book was depleting his energy. He gasped for breath, exhaustion draining down through his body, the same sensation he felt when he spent too much time inside a Crystal.

The young *seer* reached to close the Book but noticed the eyes changing from gray to Zepallo's cold blue glare. Pale bony hands reached out to grab his blue robes, dragging him headfirst into the smoky pages of the Book.

He heard Zepallo's growl, as he plunged into a roiling black void, "There are some things a young *seer* should never attempt. Reading from my Book is one of them!"

Adrian curled into a ball, tumbling through a raging tempest with no sense of time or space. Rumbling thunder chased furious tangles of icy white lightning crashing through an eternal emptiness that swallowed his screams in a deafening roar.

Zepallo's laughter blared above the din, "There's no one to hear you, let alone save you!"

A wedge of giant ravens dove on the boy with talons flared, their eyes blazing golden beacons in the murky swirling vapors. Smothering him in flapping wings and screeching terror, the huge birds lunged to peck and tear at his robes, jostling to shred bare flesh, until a brilliant flash scattered them into the squall. He plunged through the vicious storm, dropped into the jaws of a massive serpent, through rows of glistening teeth and streams of sour saliva, down a slimy caustic gullet, and out into the abyss again.

Zepallo's cruel whisper hissed, "You asked my book to show you the future and now you will witness the apocalypse!"

A glistening ring appeared in the churning gloom as Adrian unfurled himself, mesmerized by the globe of Earth, a dull jewel veiled in a grimy haze, slipping into dark sky from eclipsing the sun. Jagged lightning rippled with the intensity of a million flashbulbs firing through the dark shroud obscuring the planet and gigantic orange fires glowed, here and there, black smoke billowing from the darkened capitals of the world.

"This is the Earth after the great war. In most places, civilization and governments have collapsed. The populations of the greatest cities are fleeing to the countryside, searching for any form of sustenance and shelter from the acid rain falling from titanic storms spawned by the fires. The world, as you knew it, no longer exists. History has been erased and a new civilization will rise from the ashes, under the care and nurturing of the Council of Ollapez," thundered the Dark Lord, with a sinister laugh. "Think of it, without the encumbrances of art and literature and music or the mind-numbing blather of the world's religions, the population will worship the teachings of a universal testament and bow to wisdoms and justice bestowed by the Dark Lord. For the first time in history, everyone everywhere will worship our truth, as citizens of the new global order."

Volcanoes erupted along the junctions of the tectonic plates and hurricanes swirled across the oceans in a parade of colossal pinwheels. Monster tornadoes erupted from storms ravaging the continents in a swirling dance of death and destruction. Icebergs clogged the seas near the poles, raising the tides hundreds of feet above normal, pushing brackish water far inland along every coast.

The clouds dispersed and the remnants of the great cities appeared as smoldering skeletons of their former splendor. The streets were empty of traffic, or people walking along the sidewalks, or children playing, and there was no evidence of the bustle of urban life, as it persisted for thousands of years. Once thriving, churning metropolitan centers were deserted, save black-robed sentinels marching in regimented columns, searching to purge any pockets of resistance. Loud speakers blared, "You will march with us or you will be eliminated!"

Starving citizens, concealed in subterranean sewers, cellars, and tunnels, fell in behind the troops and struggled to keep up. In desperation, parents abandoned their children along the gutters and were instantly clothed in the black robes of the Dark Forces, as they joined the pounding cadence of the procession. Screaming children were collected by a second squadron and transported in black buses to schools, where they would be indoctrinated into a dark world order and raised to become loyal soldiers for the Council.

The vision dissolved into the conical mountain on the Island of the Children erupting with violent explosions. Deep orange lava flowed across the island, enveloping the pyramid and the plaza, surging through the tunnels to clog the underworld and entomb the Red Crystal, ensuring no survivors.

Morgan's Knot appeared and Adrian moaned helplessly, as herds of animals fled across lush fields to the beaches to protect his family and friends, just ahead of a firestorm racing across the island. Fifty or sixty *seers* flew in loose formation through charcoal clouds to confront hundreds of dark warriors riding giant black ravens in a massive assault over the ridgeline. A blazing barrage of charges flew from one side to the other, annihilating waves of fighters, until only a handful of Zepallo's guards endured. The few remaining Positive Crystals exploded, with enormous eruptions of golden sparks and embers flaring into firestorms. One by one, the positive vectors dimmed and disappeared, leaving only shimmering blue-black arrays buzzing across the planet.

~

Adrian's mother peaked around the edge of his door to find him slumped over a strange black book, his forehead resting on the pages of the metallic journal.

Sara tiptoed across the room and slowly pulled the book away. It was cold and heavy and the pages appeared to be covered with billowing smoke. Her hand tingled with dark static, as she closed the cover and placed it on his night table, before rolling her son back onto his pillows.

His forehead was cold but he was sweating profusely and did not stir as she moved him. Sara leaned over to kiss his forehead and realized that his breathing was very shallow. She shook him but his body was limp and his eyes rolled back into this skull.

In a panic, she rushed downstairs to tell the rest of the family about Adrian's condition and called Dr. Stevens on the *messenger* in George's study. "Please come quickly, Adrian is unconscious and I can't wake him!"

"I'll be there in a few minutes," replied the Doctor.

As an afterthought, she dialed Ponte.

"Ah, Sara, how are you?" The Professor's smile deflated, "You look worried, what's wrong?"

"Adrian's unconscious and I can't wake him. He was reading from a strange black, metallic book."

"A Black Book?"

"Yes. I don't know where he got it!"

"I'll call Alius and we'll be there directly."

Alius flew through the vectors to the observatory and landed on the front stoop, just as the Professor opened the door. "I know we're not supposed to use the vectors but, if you'll grant me permission, it'll be even faster and probably safer than your red trolley."

"Alright, let's go," replied Ponte. "Sara said that Adrian was reading from a black metallic book. Do you know anything about this?"

Alius gasped, "Oh my, I saw him pick up a black book, while we were in Zepallo's command center. I'd forgotten all about it, until you mentioned it."

"If he's been reading from Zepallo's Black Book, this is far more serious than I might have hoped!"

Alius placed her hand on the Professor's shoulder and zipped along the vectors, landing near the garden at the House of the Four Seasons. They rushed into the gray stone farmhouse and up the stairs to Adrian's room, where they found an anxious family gathered.

Dr. Stevens leaned over Adrian, listening to his heart, "He's just barely breathing and his pulse is extremely slow. He's running a fever but this is not like an infection that we might expect in children. I don't know what's wrong with him!"

"I think this might be the result of exposure to the dark energies," said Ponte quietly, padding across the room to Adrian's bed to pick up the Black Book from the nightstand. He opened the cover and stared at the smoky pages. "Now I'm certain that this is not a medical condition."

Alius whispered, "It's steeped in the dark energies. I felt the chill, when we entered this room."

Sara slumped against Adrian's father, John, and gasped, "Oh, no!"

Dr. Stevens ripped the top sheet off the bed and tossed it to Elsie, who was standing with George near the door. Soak this in cold water! At the very least, we have to try to get his temperature down before the fever causes brain damage!"

Elsie rushed into the bathroom, stuffed the sheet into the tub and ran cold water until it was sopping wet. The Doctor tore off Adrian's robes and his Aunt bustled across the bedroom to wrap the sheet around the young *seer*.

"I think we're going to need some help from our fellow *seers*," exclaimed Alius, escaping through the darkened hallway, down the stairs, and out the kitchen door to sit on the steps, bawling. She closed her eyes and concentrated on Simian, Raffe, and Mary, "If you can hear me, we need your help and we need you now!"

She took a deep breath and settled herself, forcing her respiration to become light and shallow, crossed her legs, and commanded her body to feel as light as a feather. Slowly, the little *seer* rose a foot above the steps and, in deep meditation, cleared her mind of everything except the Thai *seer*, Sky. In the depths of her consciousness, she pleaded with the tiny woman. "I know you can hear me. I know you're aware. Please come quickly, Adrian's dying!"

Alius was startled out of her state, as Simian materialized beside her. "I felt you through the vectors. What's wrong?"

"It's Adrian. Evidently, he was reading from Zepallo's Black Book. He's unconscious and I think he's dying!"

The old Jamaican wrapped his arms around the beautiful young *seer*, "I promise that we will find a way to save him."

With a kiss to her cheek, he raced up the steps and disappeared through the kitchen door. Alius tried to concentrate but it was no use. She buried her face in her hands and wept.

A soft touch on her shoulder roused her and she looked up into Mary's gentle eyes and Raffe leaning in behind her. "What's happened?

We both felt a disturbance and knew something was happening on Morgan's Knot. We got here as fast as we could."

"Thank you for coming. It's Adrian. We think that he was reading from Zepallo's Black Book and he's unconscious. Dr. Stevens is with him but the Professor thinks that this isn't a medical condition!"

Without a word, Raffe ran up the steps, while Mary sat down beside Alius and wrapped her arms around the girl, who buried her face in Mary's shoulder and sobbed.

Suddenly, the air stirred and a glow appeared at the bottom of the steps. Alius looked up into the enchantment of Sky's soft smile. She could not restrain her relief and stood to absorb the warmth of the tiny woman's aura, "Thank you for coming. Adrian was reading from Zepallo's Book and he's unconscious."

Sky hugged her and looked up at Mary, "This is serious. He's suspended in the dimension of the dark energies. Zepallo tried to control Raffe's mind, now he's stolen Adrian's spirit!"

The three women rushed through the kitchen and climbed the stairs to Adrian's room. Molly and Megan were hugging in the doorway, weeping. They shuffled aside to allow the three *seers* to enter. John was trying to hug an inconsolable Sara, who was kneeling next to the bed, sobbing into Adrian's pillow. Dr. Stevens, usually calm and composed, looked helpless, and Ponte was absently drumming his fingers on the cover of the Black Book.

Alius introduced Sky to everyone in the room. The tiny woman walked over to the bed and brushed her hand across Adrian's forehead. She lifted his eyelids and peered into his lifeless stare. Finally, she placed her hand on his chest and felt his heart beating very slowly.

Turning back to the group, who were staring anxiously, she said, "He's been pulled into another dimension. It's a dark plane that sustains the world of the Legio Obscurum. Several of you accompanied me to the plane of the animals. While that wonder represents everything good in nature, this dimension is the embodiment of everything evil in the world."

"The good news is that Adrian will not die, at least not as long as Zepallo and his comrades can use his energy, his spark of life. For the moment, he will remain in this state."

Sara wiped her eyes, "Can we get him back?"

"I don't know but we'll try," said the Thai *seer*, kneeling to wrap her arms around Adrian's mother. Sky looked around the room and paused, for a moment, to stare into each *seer's* eyes. "We will try."

~

Zepallo leaned back in his chair, enthralled with the smoky apparition spinning above the center of the round table. He gazed around at the twelve Ministers of the Council of Ollapez, "This is lightning in a bottle. If he's allowed to live in his world, he'll become the most powerful and dominating *seer* on the planet. As it is, we have only to find a way to transform his energy into something useful."

"In its present state, his spirit and energy will only live as long as his body remains alive," sneered Wonac, the hulking Dark Master and Minister of Military Affairs, sitting across the table from Zepallo, waving his hand at the swirling golden mist, which quivered at the stroke in the calm air.

"I can promise you that his family and friends on Morgan's Knot will do everything in their power to maintain his life. He's a hero and a savior in their eyes."

"Perhaps it would be easier to just let him die," snarled Ptolemy, an ancient and domineering dark *seer* and Minister of State with a gray beard that swung back and forth like moldy fog as he spoke.

"You miss the point, Master. I've battled with this *seer* several times. He's responsible for connecting all of the nodes, the destruction of our facilities on Ice Island, and the more recent embarrassment in New York. He led the animals into the United Nations and revealed the promise of the Balance to the real world. The young prince possesses an energy that goes far beyond anything that any of us have ever encountered in our campaigns against the Forces of the Light. This *seer* has the potential to unite them in triumph." Pointing to the spinning haze, he added, "Look at this little cloud. It glows with life, with power and potential. It is truly unique in all the planes. We must consult the texts!"

With that, he opened a small black *orb*, exposing a central core that pulsed with a scalding deep red glow. He nudged it beneath the golden cloud, gently sucked the haze inside, twisted it closed, and placed it at the center of the table, before he stood.

"Let us endeavor to discover a means to not only control this energy, but to use it for our purposes. Each of us should delve into the deepest chapters of the Dark Texts. This is a treasure and an opportunity that only comes along once. I would suggest that, if we are clever, turning his spirit could lead to a final triumph. Let us begin!"

Ptolemy did not stand but gazed across the circular table at Zepallo impatiently. His old eyes blazed with indignation at the brash upstart's brazen audacity, "The Council has acquiesced to your ambitions in the past and suffered severe losses. The existence of our society has been revealed for the first time in history and this *child* played you for the fool in front of a worldwide audience. The Masters have agreed to our path and we will proceed. If we can find a way to use this energy to our benefit, fine. If not, then we will dispose of this problem, so we can move on to the next phase of our campaign. There is much to do and we have little time to waste."

Zepallo fingered the black *orb* on the table. "The fact that this boy-*seer* found the means to defy my stature should stand as reason enough to pursue this matter. Although he is young, I respect his power. We must find a way to turn him to our advantage."

Adrian realized that he lacked his five senses and, yet, he was aware of smoky rage drifting around the cavern. It was not that he could actually see or hear but, somehow, he sensed tensions flaring in the tangle of auras flailing around him. Deep murmurs and fiery emotions pummeled his consciousness, like cranky patrons arguing in whispers, haggling over a priceless piece of art in some hallowed museum.

He felt the sensations of his body, while grasping that he was barely connected to the living corpse, lying on his bed in The House of the Four Seasons, desperately clinging to life. With every ounce of concentration, he tried to will himself back to his home…to himself, but he knew that he was trapped in this strange and terrifying dimension. He thought about his fellow *seers* and wondered whether they were aware of his current state. He saw visions of Alius smiling, her white hair flowing around blue eyes glistening with her perceptive glint. Mary and Raffe appeared in blue robes and Simian, peeking over his little glasses, laughing with his entire being.

Suddenly, all of his friends joined hands in a circle. Sky was talking to the group in gentle soothing tones, guiding them toward total concentration. He imagined standing in the middle of the ring, turning slowly, staring into their eyes, one by one. He felt they were trying to find him and he gathered all of his energy in an effort to respond. "I'm a hostage in this strange suspended state. Please come for me, I want to go home!"

His essence swirled into a tight whirling funnel, as his energy was drawn into a fierce red glow, and then there was silence.

~

Sky led the *seers* into the cold night air and arranged them a circle, pointing to ignite a blazing fire that erupted from the frozen ground to warm them. They joined hands, as she spoke very softly, "Concentrate on Adrian's energy. We've all felt it. It's very strong. See him in your heart and allow your spirit to explore the dimensions. He's out there somewhere and we will find him."

The *seers* closed their eyes, as Sky whispered, "Adrian we know you're out there. We're trying to find you. Speak to us."

After a few moments, Alius' eyes opened wide, "I hear him. He wants to come home!"

Sky's voice barely whispered, "Listen again, where is his voice coming from?"

Alius retreated to her meditation, whispering, "It's far away, like a voice echoing from a great distance through a tunnel. In a way, it sounds muted, like sound traveling through water. It's not his voice, yet I know it is. Does that make any sense?"

"Yes, it does," smiled Sky. "If you had to point to it, which direction is it coming from?"

Alius raised her hand, wavering between east and southeast. Suddenly, she frowned, "It's gone."

Ponte stood in the doorway to the kitchen, hesitant to interrupt their séance. He plodded down the steps, to stand before the group and address Sky, "I am Professor Ponte, Keeper of the Powers on Morgan's Knot. We've developed a system that allows us to monitor the vectors, all of the vectors. I don't know whether it would be of any help, but perhaps we could get a fix on the location of their lair by watching for disruptions in the dark vectors. If Alius is correct, we should begin that search by looking in a band between east and southeast."

"That's a place to begin," replied Sky. "Adrian's body is in good hands and, other than moral support, there's nothing more we can do to help here. I would suggest that all of you accompany The Professor and search the vectors and the Books for any hint of their location. There are some people that I must see but I promise, I'll be back in a little while."

With that, she bowed her head and vanished.

The four *seers* surrounded Ponte to flash across the island, landing in the parlor of the observatory and startling Ester, who was standing in front of a feeble fire in a lavender housecoat, fuzzy pink slippers peeking from beneath the hem and her silver hair sprouting from a floppy knitted cap.

"What's happening? I awoke up to find you gone and now you appear with all of the *seers*…but where's Adrian?"

Ponte walked over and wrapped his plump arms around his tall slender wife, "Adrian was reading from Zepallo's Black Book. We think the Dark Lord has stolen his spirit. His body is lying in his bed and he is just barely alive."

"Oh, my," gasped Ester, tears welling in her eyes. "We must find a way to get him back!"

Alius and Mary joined the hug, "That's why we're all here. We just left Sky and she's gone to find more help. For the moment, we have to use all of our powers to try to find Adrian."

Alius pulled away to follow Raffe into the dining room to open the Books, as Ponte kissed his wife's cheek and turned to power up the *messengers*, "Ester would you put on some coffee? And make it strong!"

Chapter Two

Sky landed on a sandy beach in a little bay with a view over Ukora Island to the vast indigo expanse of Lake Victoria beyond. The sun was rising over her shoulder and the light glittered across the surface of the water in tiny explosions of silver and gold. She paused for a moment to open herself to the lush beauty, sensing countless birds and animals stirring night into day.

Adrian had the potential to be the most powerful *seer* that she had ever met. In spite of the depth of her own talents, she knew he possessed the spirit and magnetism to lead those who believed in the Balance to victory over the Dark Forces.

She thought back to the years spent as a timid student of the old monk, Mantis. He had taught her many things about the magic of the Light, shown her the wonders of the Balance of Nature, and instructed her in the ways of a Master *seer*.

The one question that she asked repeatedly, echoed through her memories, "Are there *seers* who rise into a state of understanding, a consciousness above the level of the Master *Seer*?"

She could hear his deep melodic voice, "First, we both know that there is no end to the learning, no point where either of us will know enough. There is always more and, certainly, we are riddled with imperfections and vanities that will need rectification for the rest of our lives." The delight in his eyes disappeared, "Once in a millennia, a *seer* is born who has the ability to unite our tribes in the war against the Legio Obscurum. They're very rare and there hasn't been one of the 'special ones', to relieve the burden of our spiritual mother, through many generations. That's one of the reasons that the Dark Forces are gaining power and influence across the planet."

"If I meet one of the 'special ones,' how will I know?"

The old *seer* laughed and laughed, before the smile deflated and he peered deeply into her eyes, "I searched for many years before I found you and I knew the moment our auras touched. You're developing into a very powerful *seer* and you are certainly very special in so many ways. If you find the 'one', you will know and I hope you will teach and guide this person in the things I've taught you. The survival of our world will depend on both of you."

Sky was warmed by the wisdom of her mentor. Although his death, at the hands of a marauding squad of dark *seers,* was indelibly etched in her memory, she found that she carried his laughter and kindness in her heart. Mantis allowed her to see the world through his eyes, without a veil to conceal the horrors that occurred throughout history, balanced by his absolute delight in the wonders of nature and the goodness that glows in the eyes of every newborn creature. He saw all the dimensions, light and dark, and guided her to his belief that the evils in the world were merely obstacles in the path to a true equilibrium. They represented the work of the *seer,* the challenges that had yet to be overcome, and the goal of a lifelong struggle. She missed him.

Turning up a narrow path, she marched into a tiny village high on a bluff overlooking the lake. She found Shambala surrounded by a herd of young children, all smiling and laughing. Sky was always amazed to watch the beautiful young woman untangle herself to stand. She was more than six feet tall and very slender, with huge dark eyes that always shimmered with compassion and warmth. Her hair was cropped close to her head and she wore clusters of bracelets of silver and gold around her wrists and ankles that jangled as she walked.

Shambala broke into a smile and ran to lift her friend off the ground in a hug. "I sensed that you were near! It's been so long since your last visit!"

"I know and I do apologize," replied Sky, as the giant girl placed her back on the ground, with a kiss on each cheek. "I need your help."

A gaggle of children gathered around to hug Sky, hoping for the treats that were usually hidden in her vibrant yellow robes. "I'm afraid that I don't have anything for you this time, but I promise to bring something special the next time I come to see you."

The children dispersed with disappointed moans but one tiny girl remained, standing with her hands behind her back.

"You always bring us surprises. This time I have something for you!" she said, holding out a flower with waxy burgundy petals surrounding a brilliant orange pincushion of tendrils. "We call it a Paintbrush Lily."

Sky accepted the gift with a gentle smile and tucked it behind her ear. "Thank you, Mambazi. You've brightened my day, so I'll carry it with me to remind me of your beautiful smile!"

The young girl giggled and wandered away to play with her friends. The two women walked to a shady spot beneath a giant fig tree and sat on woven grass mats. "I'm not used to this expression that you are wearing on your face," said Shambala. "What's wrong?"

"Did you hear of the confrontation at the United Nations?"

"Yes," laughed the tall woman, "but the drummers had a hard time translating the whale mail version that described all the animals that filled the aisles!"

Sky smiled, "Well, the young *seer* who orchestrated that show has been kidnapped by Zepallo. It isn't so much that he was kidnapped, the Evil One stole his spirit."

Shambala gasped, "How did the Dark Lord separate his essence from his body?"

"The young *seer*, Adrian, managed to pick up Zepallo's Black Book, while he and his friends were destroying the Dark Forces' bunker in New York, and made the mistake of reading from it without protection or supervision. When I arrived, his body was just barely alive, but his spirit was gone."

"There's more to this than you're telling me."

"When Mantis was training me, he often spoke of that one special *seer* who comes along once in a millennia, the one with the strength and the vision to lead the rest of us to defeat Legio Obscurum. This young man is the one."

Shambala's graceful finger touched her lip, "Are you sure?"

"I'm certain and we must find a way to get him back. He's in a dark dimension and undoubtedly under their control. You're one of the few *seers* in the world who understands the movements of the planes, which is why I came to you first. I need your help and your knowledge," said Sky quietly.

"You, of all people, know the dangers of moving about within the dark planes," sighed the tall woman, as she adjusted her long legs beneath her. "We'll need more *seers* to add energy and expertise to this effort."

Sky smiled, "There are four, very dedicated *seers* waiting to hear from me and I'm going to see Master Chi and Lala and Maze before I return to them. Although I haven't developed a plan, I know that, if we join together, we'll find a way."

"What else can you tell me about this young *seer*?"

"He's confronted Zepallo several times and, in each case, succeeded in driving the Dark Lord back. He and his friends were the ones who connected all of the nodes together, destroyed their facilities on Ice Island, and, as I said, organized the confrontation in the United Nations."

"I didn't realize that one person was behind these triumphs," smiled Shambala. "I'm impressed and I can see why you think that he's the one."

"While we've been working in isolation, the Dark Forces have grown in strength and organization and I have no doubt that they're building towards a final confrontation. If they can turn Adrian's spirit and energy to their cause, they might just win."

"If this young man is as strong as you believe, then it will take them a while to turn his light to darkness. We must find a way to retrieve him before they find a solution to the problem."

Sky was silent for a moment, focusing on a cluster of white orchids with deep purple throats and vibrant golden anthers. "I agree. If you're willing to help, stay open and I'll call to you when I've gathered enough friends to our cause. It won't be long."

"I'll await your call and, in the meantime, consider our options and gather my students," smiled the beautiful black woman. She took Sky's hand in hers and squeezed it gently. "Mantis would be very proud of you."

"Thank you," replied the tiny Thai *seer*. "It's time for me to go."

The two women stood and hugged, "Be safe on your journey."

"I'll get back to you as soon as we're ready," said Sky softly, as she gathered her robes around her body and lowered her head. A moment later, she was gone.

The little *seer* landed at the gates of a beautiful pagoda above a small village on the north slope of the Himalayas. A blizzard was howling around the hamlet but there was no snow on the tiled roof of the temple. Flowers bloomed in profusion and the dense forest of trees was lush with green foliage. No matter the season, it was always spring at the Temple of Ancient Truths.

A pool of water surrounded the shrine and offered no path to the entrance. Sky smiled, as she thought back to the first time her mentor, Mantis, brought her here to meet his Master.

As a young girl, she looked up and asked, "Is there a boat to take us to the Temple?"

He laughed and laughed before replying, "You must believe!" With that, he let go of her little hand and padded across the water to the steps leading up to the shrine. He turned around and smiled at his young charge, "Come on, you can do it. You just have to believe in the Power of the Light. You're letting your mind get in the way of your heart. Listen with your feet! They know that they can walk across this little pond. See yourself, here next to me."

Sky started to cry. She watched Mantis walk across the water but had no idea of how to follow him. Suddenly, her mentor was standing beside her. He knelt down and wiped the tears from her cheeks, "You are a fine young *seer*. Sometimes, you have to let go of the things that you know to be true and accept the idea that there are many possibilities in every situation. Can humans fly? No, but we can move through the vectors. We can travel through the planes to visit the animals. Soon, you will learn to levitate yourself and move around like a little cloud. This is one of those things. You just have to believe that you can do it and you will find that you can. Come, give me your hand and we'll walk together."

Sky grasped his strong hand, took a deep breath, and stepped off the bank of the pool beneath the gates. Mantis whispered, "Do not look at your feet, they know where they're going. Look ahead to where you want to be."

The young *seer* concentrated on the steps leading up to the entrance of the shrine and visualized herself standing there. A moment later, they stepped onto the bank of the pond and she looked up at Mantis with a huge smile. The sound of his laughter, in that moment, allowed her to see that she could overcome her own fears and she never again retreated from a challenge.

She walked across the pool of cold clear water, followed by a school of Koi trolling through the cascade of circular ripples radiating from her steps, and climbed the wooden stairs, smoothed by the bare feet of thousands of young monks and worshippers, who entered the ornate entry over the centuries. Before she reached the top step, the doors opened, revealing a slender old monk in saffron robes. His head was cleanly shaven and his eyes sparkled with the innocent glee of a mischievous child.

He placed the palms of his hands together and bowed to the tiny *seer*, "Madame Sky, it has been a long time since your last visit. I am pleased to see you!"

"And I am pleased to be here, Master Jung. Is our Master in the temple?"

"He is and he's expecting you. If you will follow me, I'll take you to him," said the monk, holding the door to allow her to enter.

He turned to his right into a tall narrow hallway that stretched away from the foyer and she noticed that his steps were so light and fluid that he appeared to float above the polished wooden planks in the floor. He was, not only, a revered monk but also Keeper of the Powers for this tiny island of hope. They turned into an alcove on the left and stopped before a plank door, its cherry lacquered patina long since worn from the grain in the teak. Before the monk could knock, a soft voice bellowed, "Please come in Sky, I've been expecting you!"

The monk smiled and bowed, as Sky entered the room and the door closed silently behind her. The Master was seated on a small, beautiful carpet surrounded by hundreds of flickering candles. Incense filled the room with sweet smog billowing through the soft light.

"Please sit down," smiled Master Chi. "It has been a long time since your last visit. To what do we owe this honor?"

"You are the Master and you knew that I was coming, so I must assume that you already know!" laughed the tiny *seer*, as she settled on the carpet, facing the old man. His head was shiny bald and a slender gray patch of beard fell from his chin. His dark knowing eyes twinkled in the candlelight and his smile conveyed an inner peace and wisdom that seemed at odds with his reputation as a prankster.

"You are here on serious business, although I'm not sure what puzzle you've brought for me to solve!"

"You're right. It is serious business but, first, I should apologize for not coming to see you more often."

"I could chastise you but it would do no good, I know you too well!" laughed the old man, his round stomach jiggling in his merriment. "The important element is that you always return exactly when you're supposed to."

"I come to you because, long ago, Mantis told me that, if I ever needed advice or guidance, you were not only his friend and mentor but the wisest monk that he had ever known."

"I taught him well and he taught you. I am honored that you thought of me."

The tiny *seer* blushed, "I come to you with an unusual problem," she began.

The old monk held up his hand for silence, "You have found the one!"

Sky pouted, "How do you know these things?"

"I can see through all the dimensions of our world!" The Master's old face crinkled into a warm smile, his eyes glistening with glee, "Actually, it is in your eyes but there's something else there. You're troubled about this person. How can I help you?"

"If you will indulge me for a few minutes, I'll explain it to you."

"As you wish," cackled the monk.

"You've heard about the *seers* who connected all of the nodes together?"

"Yes, I heard that tale and I am aware of a smoothness in the vectors. We can travel through the paths without going 'bump' when we pass through the Crystals."

"Have you heard about the confrontation at the United Nations?"

"Word reached us, through the whale mail, that a group of *seers* disrupted a speech by that scoundrel, Zepallo, and introduced the Ambassadors to the Balance in a rather entertaining manner."

"The young *seer* that I come to you about is the one who accomplished these things and more. I'm convinced that he is the 'one' that Mantis told me about. He said that a special *seer* comes along very rarely but I would know, if I ever met that person."

The eyes of the old Monk were focused, absorbing every word, and Sky felt that his mind was connected to her soul and open to her truth.

"Unfortunately, while this young *seer* was destroying the Dark Lord's lair, he picked up a Black Book and made the mistake of reading from it without supervision. In the process, Zepallo stole his spirit. His body is barely alive and his essence has disappeared. I believe the Dark

Forces will try to turn his energy to their benefit and I must find a way to save him."

"If you are correct that he is the 'one' then it is imperative that we retrieve him. The last time a special one appeared, the Dark Forces were driven into a retreat that lasted for almost a thousand years. Her power and influence guide us to this day but the dark cloud is, again, spreading across the world like the web of their dark vectors and we both know that their goal remains the same. We are approaching a cataclysm and the future of the Balance may well be at stake."

The monk closed his eyes and was silent for several minutes. "The answer that you seek comes from the inner character of this young man. He has provided you with the path to his own salvation."

"I've only met this boy once but I was struck by the same strengths that I admire in you - his innocence, strength, and dedication to the Balance and the Powers of the Light. His accomplishments show that he is clever, inventive, and he's risked his life more than once. From what I understand, his solutions to the confrontations he's faced were anything but obvious."

The old monk smiled, "You have just reached your first conclusion. The answer to this puzzle will not be simple or apparent. This young *seer* would not see this challenge as an iron gate that must be torn down. He might see it as billowing, shimmering silk that must be brushed aside with a most gentle touch."

Sky was quiet for a moment, as she considered his advice. "I can see there are questions that I must ask of those who are closest to him but what you are saying is that he would not necessarily mount a full frontal assault. He would find a more subtle way to achieve his goal."

"You are correct! Perhaps a direct challenge is the best answer but your friend would consider every possibility before deciding on his course of action." laughed the old monk. His dark eyes turned cold, "You realize that there is one other alternative that must be considered, if the Dark Forces do turn his spirit?"

The tiny Thai woman looked deeply into the old man's eyes. "I don't think I want to understand what you're saying," she whispered.

"If his body dies, his spirit will die with it," said the old monk, quietly.

"That can not be an alternative," said Sky, adamantly.

"I was hoping you would offer that reply. As you pointed out, this young *seer* did not always seek the easiest solutions to the challenges he has faced, he chose the correct ones. Now it is up to you to find the appropriate path to rescuing this young *seer*."

"May I ask for your help, when I find a way to mount this campaign?"

"I am at your service and have at least a dozen *seers*-in-training, who might prove most helpful," said the old monk, as he bowed to the tiny *seer*.

Sky stood and placed her palms together, "I appreciate your counsel. I'll let you know when we're ready."

The old monk rose slowly and took both her hands in his, "This is a necessary but dangerous undertaking. The future of the world might well depend on your success."

Sky bowed her head. "It will not be my success but ours."

The monk's old eyes scrunched into a kind smile.

~

The tiny *seer* pondered the old sage's advice, as she slipped through the vectors, hardly noticing the streaming colors or the low hum that flowed around her. Suddenly, she was standing on a rocky beach along the twisted shoreline of Isla de los Estados, a tiny island at the southern tip of South America. A fierce biting gale rushed in from the ocean and a dozen seagulls hovered, motionless, staring down curiously. Perhaps they thought her saffron robes held the promise of a colossal treat.

Sky walked slowly along a carpet of smooth pebbles covering the beach, until she found a path winding up through a forest of small gnarled trees, twisted and bent but standing determined against relentless winds. She approached an ancient village, where smoke rose from round stone huts with sturdy thatched roofs erected in concentric circles surrounding a smooth plaza for tribal gatherings. Several small children ran to greet and guide her to the largest shelter on the south side of the inner circle.

A heavy tarp was pulled away to reveal the deeply wrinkled face of a very old, tiny man with a fluffy white beard and a crooked little hat. Huge dark eyes twinkled, as he gestured for her to enter. A small fire burned brightly at the center of the room and an old woman was busy stirring the contents of a large pot, hanging from a chain attached to a steel hook secured to the beams supporting the ceiling. She was smaller than Sky.

The ancient shaman dropped her spoon and wrapped Sky in a warm embrace, "It's so nice to see you. It's been much too long!"

"That's my fault, Lala," replied Sky. "I apologize for not coming to visit more often and for arriving without warning you."

"You know you're always welcome here but I sense that you've come for some other reason than to make up for your absence."

"You are always correct. I'm here seeking help."

"Then you've come to the right place," replied the old woman. "Please, come sit by the fire. You must be cold."

"When I was studying with Mantis, he told me that once in a millennium, a special *seer* comes along who has the power to lead the Forces of the Light against the Legio Obscurum. I believe that I've met that person."

"Oh, that's wonderful. We all sense that the Dark Powers are swelling."

"Unfortunately, he's young and made a dire mistake. You might have heard about the show at the United Nations?"

"We heard about that through the whale mail, I haven't laughed so hard in a very long time!"

"Well…while this young man was in Zepallo's warren, he picked up a Black Book and attempted to read from it without understanding the danger. His body isn't really alive but not quite dead either, and his spirit has been stolen by the Evil Ones. I believe that everything depends on getting him back."

"That is a conundrum," said the old woman, stirring the pot that emitted an intoxicating aroma of garlic and rosemary.

"There are four *seers* waiting for my return to Morgan's Knot, the island where this young *seer* lives. I've also been to see Shambala and Master Chi and I'm here to ask for your help and guidance."

"You know that we'll do whatever we can to help you in this cause."

Maze, the old man, had been hovering silently in the shadows, "We must join together against the Dark Forces. If your intuition about this young man is correct, then the future of the Balance is at stake. What can we do?"

"Master Chi suggested that the answer to this challenge must come from the personality of Adrian, the missing *seer*. I don't yet know him well enough to see a solution. I'll talk with his fellow *seers* and his friends and family but I would ask that you be ready when we have formed a plan."

"You know we'll do whatever we can to help," responded the old woman through the haze billowing above the boiling pot. "Just let us know."

"Thank you," said Sky, quietly. "I know there's a strategy, I just can't see it yet."

Maze cackled, "Anyplace else is warmer than here but we aren't going anywhere until we hear from you!'"

Sky rose and hugged the old couple, bowed her head, and vanished. Maze walked over and leaned into the smoke rising from the pot, "That'll clear your sinuses!"

"You old devil," snapped Lala, swatting him with a towel. "Go meditate. Contact our friends. We'll need their help."

Chapter Three

Alius was exhausted but desperate. The four *seers* had been probing the Texts for hours, in frustration at not finding the clues they were seeking. Ponte and Nanchez wandered back and forth between the *messengers* in the parlor and the dining room table, offering questions and avenues not yet explored, which occasionally proved worthy of consideration. The Keepers devised a filter to monitor the dark vectors but they found no disruptions that might indicate the location of the lair of the Dark Forces.

Ester pushed a small cart in from the kitchen with a crock of stew and a loaf of freshly baked bread, "All of you need a break. Put those books away and let's have some dinner!"

Without argument, Simian and Alius closed the covers of the Books and laid them on the sideboard. Mary and Raffe brought silverware and dishes from the kitchen and everyone sat down at the table.

"It's weird, trying to tackle this problem without Adrian," sighed Raffe. "He's always the first to find solutions to these puzzles or at least point us in the right direction."

Ponte reached across the table to pat Ester's hand and laughed, "I'm reminded of his plan to rescue my bride."

Nanchez grinned, "We weren't expecting an onslaught of animals and swarms of insects or pyrotechnics for that matter!"

"And the pirates," added Raffe. "They still think the Island of the Children is haunted by ghosts and aliens!"

"How about the two Crystals that were grinding together in South America? I honestly didn't think he'd survive that one," commented Simian.

"He never gives up and neither will we," sighed Alius. "We have to find a solution to get him back, before they find a way to turn his spirit to the Darkness."

Mary reached over and touched her hand, "We'll find him. I don't think any of us realized how much we depend on him, his inventive spirit, or his sense of humor!"

"Has anyone checked in with Sara?" inquired Ester.

Everyone glanced around the table without reply. They had been so engrossed in trying to find a lead, a tiny crack that they might use to their advantage, they had not considered Adrian's body, lying on his bed at the House of the Four Seasons.

"All of you have enough to do, I'll call her after we finish our meal," said Ester, answering her own question.

Everyone pitched in to clear the table and clean up the kitchen, while Ester rang up the House of the Four Seasons.

Megan appeared before the *messenger* with sad puffy eyes, "Hi, Ester, how are you?"

"I'm fine, dear. What's happening there?"

"Dr. Stevens has been here since last night but there really isn't much he can do. He knows this isn't a medical condition but he's doing everything he can to keep Adrian alive."

"I have faith in his talents and his wisdom. Is your Aunt Sara close by?"

"Yes, hang on and I'll get her."

A moment later, Sara appeared, gray shadows of worry and despair veiled her sad blue eyes, "Hello, Ester. What's happening on your end?"

"The *seers* are probing the Texts but we haven't found a solution to the problem. Little Sky left hours ago to round up allies and we haven't heard from her since. Is there anything that we can do for you?"

"Just keep trying. Adrian is still alive, if just barely. It's almost as if he's in a state of suspended animation. Dr. Stevens is applying some of his healing waters to keep him hydrated and that seems to have brought his fever down to normal. Sadly, there has been no change."

"I'm sorry, dear," sighed Ester. "We'll let you know if we find anything and you let us know if there is any improvement."

"I will," replied Sara, tears welling, "Give everyone our thanks. I know they're doing their best."

"Take care of yourself. You look tired."

"I am but I can't leave his side until we know what's happening."

"I know, dear. We'll be in touch."

Sara's image dissolved and was replaced with writhing black vectors girding the globe in a dark web of indigo filaments.

Sky landed on the path in front of the observatory as the sun was setting, firing streaks of red and orange across the heavens, a glowing celestial fan reaching for twilight. She climbed the steps to the weathered doors and knocked.

Mary opened the heavy slab and wrapped the tiny *seer* in a hug, "We were worried about you and I'm glad you're back, safe and sound."

"I've been to see some friends. We'll have help, when we need it, but I must ask all of you some questions."

"Please come and warm yourself by the fire," smiled Mary.

Everyone gathered in the parlor, as Sky stood before smoldering embers in the hearth with her hands behind her back.

Ponte was the first to speak. "We've been monitoring the dark vectors but we've not seen any movement that might give us a clue about the whereabouts of their lair. The *seers* have been combing the Books but I'm afraid we haven't found anything definitive."

"That doesn't surprise me," smiled Sky. "Have you asked about the dimensions?"

The *seers'* eyes darted one to the next, as if they had missed something obvious. "No, we haven't explored that part of it yet," sighed Alius.

"I met with the mentor of my mentor and he pointed out that the solution to our problem must come from Adrian."

"I'm afraid I don't understand," said Raffe. "We all know that Adrian is not really with us at the moment."

"It must come from his spirit, the person that he is inside," replied Sky. "The stuff that makes up the essence of his being."

Everyone was silent for a moment, before they all began talking at once. Ponte raised a chubby hand for quiet, "What you are seeking is a look inside the person that he is…or was?"

"Yes. I want to know what made him special, why he did things the way that he did, how he approached problems like this one, anything you can think of that might give us an avenue to follow."

The Professor almost whispered, "I think we should start with Alius. There's no one closer to him than you are and you've been involved with most of his adventures. You and he fought on the mountain and ended up becoming more than friends."

Alius stared at a tiny wisp of smoke rising from the fuming coals in the hearth, recalling their first encounter, "The first time we met, I tried to carve him up with a knife and he knocked me unconscious with a heavy black crystal. He could have left me to die in that blizzard but, in spite of his wounds, he carried me down the mountain and decided he'd make me understand the beauty of the Balance. I guess that's an odd way to gain a new friend but he taught me about the world that the people of the south side of the island had created over generations, through hard work, a simple belief in doing what was right, and a reverence for the animals."

"I remember the first time he took me to the forest and we were surrounded by all of the wild creatures of the island. I never had a pet, let alone met an animal who could talk, but, by the most natural magic, I was surrounded by this wonderland with squirrels, chipmunks, deer, raccoons, bears, and all sorts of birds fluttering around and he treated them as friends and equals. He showed great respect for their ideas and opinions and, in that instant, I saw the person who lives inside and he was beautiful."

"That was when our people kidnapped Ester," she continued, glancing at the woman who had taken her in and been so patient and kind. "He found the solution in the animals and he always seemed to find a way to add a little bit of humor to his plans. I wish someone had made a video of my people fleeing through the tunnels, chased by herds of animals, flocks of birds, and clouds of insects!"

"He did the same thing on the Island of the Children," interrupted Raffe. "First, he introduced all of the children to the wonders of the natural world and a very weird assortment of circus animals, who shared the island with us all along. Until he arrived, we were afraid of the animals and avoided them. He organized the children and the animals to frighten the pirates, without hurting anyone, and his plan resulted in a resolution for a problem that existed for hundreds of years."

"He saved my life…twice…once, when a shark was about to eat me and, again, in the United Nations. Even when I allowed myself to be seduced by Zepallo's lies, he never got mad, he just convinced me to see the difference between the Light and the Dark. I don't think there's an evil or malicious bone in his body but there's no stopping him when he takes a stand."

Simian laughed and continued the tale, "I've been working with him, teaching him to fly along the vectors and introducing these youngsters to levitation and seeing. His energy is very round and smooth for someone so young. He's probably the bravest person I've ever met and, yet, he doesn't seem to comprehend that he's done anything out of the ordinary."

Alius interrupted, "I know he talks with Morgan a lot and she told me that he really doesn't like the notoriety or the fame that he's earned. Even here on the island where he's surrounded by friends and family, when he's not being Adrian the *seer*, he's shy and withdrawn, and I know he'd rather just be one of the kids. He doesn't do these things because he might benefit, he does them because he knows that it's his responsibility. As he always says, 'We have no other choice.' Maybe that's what I admire most, he just does what needs to be done without hesitation, without thought for his own safety or betterment. He sees beyond the obvious solution and finds a way to solve the riddle without hurting anyone or taking anything away from them. It's almost as if he considers the bad guys as regular people who need to be enlightened. Does that make any sense?"

"Yes, it does," replied Mary. "His plan on the Island of the Children was built around the idea that no one would get hurt. He was adamant about that."

"Do you remember how he spoke of that little priest he met in the Vatican? He was so...I don't know...impressed with that man's devotion to his beliefs that he lectured us on how everyone should have the right to believe in whatever they truly believe and to be able to express those convictions," added Raffe. "I'm just learning about almost everything but I was honestly touched by his passion."

"Another thing, I've noticed about Adrian, was that he never seemed to realize that he was leading the rest of us," commented the Professor. "He treated all of us as if we were a team. He always made each of us feel that he was learning from us but, in hindsight, he was taking our thoughts and ideas and synthesizing them into something that bubbled up from someplace deep inside his mind. His plans always took the best of our ideas and turned them into something truly original, clever, and often humorous."

Ester had been quiet for a while, "I've been working with the Crystals and the Powers since I first met Ponte, as a young girl, and I've seen amazing dedication in all of you and those who came before...but I've never seen anyone work so hard for so long to find a solution to a problem. I can't tell you how many times I've had to call a halt to his efforts, just to give him a break. He wouldn't quit until someone gave him permission or he found the answer he was seeking."

"I think it's about love," whispered Simian, stroking his goatee. "He loves his family and his friends but it goes beyond that. He loves everything that the Balance represents...the animals, the people and the culture on this island, even those he's encountered on his missions. It's almost as if he opened a package and found everything important in life. He's gathered all of those things together and carries them with him wherever he goes. When he meets someone who needs one of those secrets, he shares it with them with kindness and compassion. It's as if he senses a hollow inside them and fills it with the love he carries in his heart."

"I don't think any of us could put it better," commented the Professor. "We all love and respect him but I don't think that any of us realized how he touched us, inspired us, or kept us pointed in the right direction."

Everyone was quiet, as they thought about the missing *seer*. Finally, Sky broke the silence, "What I'm hearing is that he's a very special, caring person who happens to have some fairly impressive powers and a keen sense of humor. I went to visit the teacher of my teacher and he suggested the solution to the problem would be found in the character of Adrian."

"Long ago, Mantis, the monk who instructed me, said that, once in a millennium, a special *seer* comes along who has the strength of character to stand against the Dark Forces. The last one defeated them again and again and it's taken a thousand years for them to regain their full potential. From what you've told me and the feelings I've had, during the short time I spent with Adrian, I believe that he is the 'one'."

"We all know that the Dark Forces are expanding and the time is nearing when they will attempt to dominate the Powers and then the real world. Our history leaves little doubt about the fate that awaits mankind if they succeed. With your help, Adrian led missions to connect all of the nodes, which has benefited everyone who travels along the vectors, and he exposed Zepallo, for the scoundrel that he is, in front of the whole world. He also introduced the United Nations to the concept of the Balance and we're already beginning to see the positive effects of that effort in every corner of the planet."

Ponte started laughing, "I'm sorry, I know this is serious business but I can't help myself, when I think of that scene with the Ambassadors cowering on their desks, as the animals trouped into the General Assembly."

Everyone relaxed, relieving the tension in the room.

"Where do we go from here?" inquired Raffe.

"I think we've found several important things that we should pursue," replied the tiny Thai *seer*. "First, Adrian's strength comes from his love for all of you and the animals. They've always been the energy behind his plans. Second, there are many dimensions in the world. Obviously, we live in this dimension, the plane of the positive vectors, and we just visited the plane of the animals. There are several dark dimensions that Zepallo and his comrades use, although I'm not sure how to identify the one in which Adrian is trapped. So, I think we should attempt to find out everything we can about their facilities, military strengths, and historical precedents that we might use to zero in on a location and a plan to take him back."

"I agree," said Alius, rising from her seat to place the Books on the table in the dining room. Raffe, Simian, and Mary followed and began to explore the Texts.

~

Adrian struggled to remain calm inside the black *orb* confining his energy. A deep fuming red glow, like embers hiding under ash in a dying fire, contained his essence yet, he had no sense of space. There was no up or down, no hot or cold, nothing relating to the five senses on which he relied throughout life to determine his place in the world. He felt like vapor erupting from a whistling teakettle, only to hang in the air, before condensing or wafting into the atmosphere. *"I am the ether"*, he thought. *"I'm still the person I was and yet I am nothing. I'm alive but I am not. Even if I could escape, I wonder whether the smoky haze, that I have become, would just dissipate and merge with the atoms and molecules of the atmosphere?"*

"I am free of my body yet a captive of this plane. I wonder whether this vapor could pass between the dimensions or be everywhere at once?"

His spirit explored the smooth inner surface of the globe, as he tried to will his energy back to the body barely clinging to life in his bed in the House of the Four Seasons. He could feel the warmth of his mother's embrace, see the love in her eyes, and smell the faint scent of her perfume, and he knew that she must be frantic. The memory of her smile filled him with guilt and hope. *"If I had just continued with my studies…if I'd just left the Black Book in my pouch…I could have saved her this worry. Tomorrow would have come, just like any other day, and we would all be together."*

Her endless lectures and her demand that he let her know before he took off on one of his missions echoed in the tiny confines of the *orb*, "You are my son and I want to watch you grow to be a man." His teachers had brushed on the idea of time and space and he wondered whether the dimensions held the opportunity to move around in time in the same way he had moved through the planes to travel on the vectors or visit the world of the animals.

Life is full of choices but we never know the consequences of those decisions, until we travel along that path of our lives. Going back, with the knowledge that we have gained, to unravel our mistakes almost seemed possible yet, he was a captive of Zepallo and his comrades and there was no escaping that. He had a sense that they were not sure what to do with him or, perhaps, how to use his energy to their advantage. Deep in his spirit, he knew he would resist, although he had no idea how.

He thought about his friends and wondered whether they were aware of his state. Images of each flickered though his mind. They were truly dedicated to the Balance and all that he knew to be right and true. He had great faith in their abilities and knew that Ponte and Alius would do their best to solve the puzzle but, if anyone could reach into this plane, it was little Sky. Her training extended far beyond anything that he had learned since he arrived on Morgan's Knot.

It had been less than a year, since he watched the Sparrow disappear over the horizon. That seemed another lifetime and he knew that he had been another person, a naïve and innocent child, before discovering the Powers and stumbling into his own talents. This predicament was another reminder that the mysteries and wonders of the Crystals would require complete dedication for the rest of his life, if he had a life.

The stormy dimension that he traveled through was more frightening than anything he encountered in his experience with the Powers and he wished that he could share what he learned with his friends to help in their effort to find him. He considered the first time Ponte suggested that the only way to find a solution to the dilemma of the storm on Morgan's Knot was for him to enter the Golden Crystal. It seemed impossible but he believed in his mentor and found courage.

Equus, the little monk, who dedicated his life to protecting the Crystals in The Vatican, suddenly appeared in his mind and he tried to draw strength from his example. *"He believed, so completely, in what he was doing that he had not left that chamber in decades."* His whole life was based on his beliefs and Adrian wondered whether the tiny man ever doubted the course that he had chosen. He found himself calmed by the thought that nothing could dissuade his own belief in the Powers of the Light. As he reviewed the events of the past six months, he knew he would not change anything that allowed him to become the person that he was. He heard Morgan's voice lecturing him on the fact that he could not go back to being the innocent selfish boy who had arrived on Morgan's Knot.

Images of his parents, Elsie and George, the twins, Ponte, Ester, Nanchez, Morgan, Alius, little Kelly, Ian and Josh, Raffe, Mary, and his friends on the Island of the Children floated through his mind and gave him the strength to believe that the other *seers* would find a way to retrieve him, somehow. He saw it as a race between the regimented forces that held him in this *orb* and those who might be gathered at the observatory. *"If we could find a way to free Raffe, then I know that you'll find a way to rescue me. Please hurry!"*

Chapter Four

Hours passed and the five *seers* ferreted a trove of details about the dimensions from the Texts but they still lacked that one gem that might focus their search and guide them to their friend.

Ester had been banging around in the kitchen and appeared in the doorway with a large crock of soup, "All of you have been at this for hours. It's time for a break."

The *seers* closed the books and cleared the table.

"There are plates, silverware, and a platter of sandwiches in the kitchen. Would you bring them?"

Raffe and Simian wandered into the kitchen and returned with the items requested. Everyone sat down, as Ester ladled soup into bowls and passed them around to the *seers*.

They all slumped on the table, tired and hungry, and no one spoke for minutes, the strain quelled by silence and nourishment. Finally, Ponte sat back in his chair, pushed his little glasses up the bridge of his nose with a stubby finger and said, "Let us review what we have learned."

Alius blurted, "The dimensions are fascinating. They seem to exist, like layers of an onion, in the same time and space and yet, they're isolated from each other, except in certain places where they almost seem to intersect or overlap."

Raffe added, "There seem to be seams, where one could pass from one to another."

"We haven't established the distinction between most of them," said Sky softly. "We know about the planes of the vectors, the animals, and the dark zone that Adrian has entered."

"But we still don't know how to enter that dimension or how to move around in it," interrupted Mary.

"True," replied Sky. "I'm not sure that we'll find that answer in these Books."

Ponte rubbed the crown of his bald head, "There is one Book yet to be explored."

Everyone glanced around the table before Ester spoke, "We've already lost one *seer* to that Book. I don't want to lose anyone else!"

Sky pursed her lips, "I wonder whether our combined energy might be strong enough to maintain control?"

Simian had been quietly observing for a few minutes, "We combined our energy to defeat Zepallo in South America and you used it to allow us to move together to the dimension of the animals. It's worth a try!"

Ester made that 'tsk-tsk' sound, "I have a bad feeling about this!"

"If we found the answers in the Books, we'd follow that course, but we're only finding bits and pieces, with no clear path to a solution," responded Alius. "I'm willing to try."

"Me, too," added Raffe. "We've been chasing islands in the sky, so we have to chance it because there is no better choice."

Ester's stern eyes skimmed from one to the next, "There are parts of this magic that are still beyond the knowledge and powers of exceptional *seers* and knowledgeable Keepers. This is one of them."

The *seers* cleared the dishes and Ponte brought the Black Book from the parlor and set it in the middle of the table.

"Before we begin, I think all of us should ground ourselves in the Balance. We know the Light is stronger than the Dark and, if we ever needed that strength, this might be the moment," instructed the tiny Thai *seer*.

The seers settled into a state of openness and caution.

"Let us join hands," said Sky quietly.

Ponte leaned over the table and opened the black metallic cover to reveal the smoky pages. A chill filled the room and two vacuous eyes appeared in the Book.

"We seek information about the dark dimension," whispered Alius, straining to focus on the subtle movement and changes in the eyes. She was cold and felt her strength draining, a slow steady drip marking the limitations of this endeavor.

"The dark planes reach every corner of the planet and far beyond."

"Is there a entry point?" inquired Simian.

"There are many transits."

"Ask if there is central location for the Dark Forces," injected the Professor.

"Where is the lair of the Dark Forces," asked Mary.

"There are many."

"We seek their primary location."

The eyes in the Book stared back at the *seers*. It seemed to be judging their strength. "All of the Books are programmed to respond with truthful answers to your questions but I sense that you do not dwell in the dark light."

"Answer the question," demanded Alius.

"The current operational command center is beneath a lake in the Caucasus Mountains."

"That might explain some of the tragedies that have occurred in those countries over the centuries," whispered Ester.

"Is there an entry from the surface?" asked Raffe.

"No. It can only be reached through one of several dimensions."

"I sense that you are being deceptive!"

"As I said, the fortress is beneath a lake."

"Do the entry points lead to that dimension?"

"Yes but they also lead to others."

"What is the distinction?" inquired Sky.

"The dark energies extend through three levels. The first is pure energy that generates violent storms, earthquakes, and volcanoes, and fuels the Dark Powers. The second is the plane of the dark vectors and the third is useful for communications and transportation."

"Now we know how that hurricane was spawned," commented Simian. "Is anyone else feeling their energy being drained away?"

Mary was beginning to look pale and faint, "Yes, I am."

Simian scanned around the table and noticed that Sky was the only one who appeared to be maintaining her state of concentration. "I know we haven't found all of the answers that we are seeking but I'm beginning to sense a danger."

"I agree," said the tiny *seer*, reaching out to close the Book. "I think we understand what happened to Adrian. He kept going, even though he knew his powers were being diminished by the negative energy of that book."

Alius slumped over with her forehead on the table. "That's exhausting," she moaned, "and I thought reading from the Silver Book or entering the Crystals took a lot of energy!"

Raffe leaned back in his chair, his head tilted to stare at the ceiling, "I felt as if someone was trying to pull my guts out!"

"I think all of you deserve a rest," said Ester. "Please, let's leave this for a little while."

"I agree," said Sky, standing to wander into the parlor, where Nanchez was working on one of the *messengers*.

Raffe suddenly sat upright in his chair, "I just thought of something that might be important. Simian, do you remember the black pendant that you removed while we were in the General Assembly?"

"I do," replied the old Jamaican.

"Zepallo showed me this book," he continued, tapping the cover the Black Book. "He said that the black crystal would protect me and I didn't feel my energy being drained away, even though I was still his zombie."

"I wonder whether it absorbs the negative waves produced by their book?"

"That's an interesting point," smiled Nanchez, pulling a pendant from beneath his shirt. "Was it like this?"

Simian and Raffe both responded at the same time, "Yes, it was exactly like that!"

Nanchez held up the black crystal for everyone to see, "Everyone in close proximity to the Black Crystal wears one of these. It seems to negate the influence of the dark energies."

"I usually wear one, when I'm reading from the Silver Book, but even with that protection this book is exhausting," said Alius, fingering the black stone suspended from a thin chain around her neck. "I think everyone should have one, if we attempt a rescue in their lair."

"I can provide them for each of you," said Nanchez, dropping the pendant beneath his shirt. "Now, let's see what happens when we focus our filters on the Caucasus."

The worldview zoomed in on a mountainous region in southern Europe. A tangle of dark vectors arced from a circle of peaks surrounding a large lake. "Now, that's interesting!"

Everyone gathered around the glowing monitor, mesmerized by the plot floating in front of the *orb*.

"Everything seems to be quiet at the moment," commented Ponte. "We'll have to keep an eye out to see if there are any movements."

"I've been thinking about something that Alius said earlier. It was something about where the planes seem to overlap or intersect each other," pondered Sky. "I wonder whether it's possible to move between the dimensions at those points?"

"Didn't you take us from the plane of the positive vectors to the plane of the animals?" asked Raffe.

"Yes, we did move from one to another," replied the little woman, "but they're both positive. My question is whether the positive and the negative touch each other in places, where we might be able to enter the dark vectors closer to our destination."

"I'm not sure that you'll find the answer in the Book of Wisdoms," commented Ponte.

Nanchez looked at Ponte, "I've worked with the dark vectors since I was a boy but I have to admit that I had no idea of these additional planes of energy. We used them, without really understanding them, for communications, power, and domestic functions. In hindsight, I guess we tapped into one of the other dark dimensions to create the storm over the island and I wonder whether we might use that system to explore the points where the planes overlap."

"You might be on to something," replied the Professor with a smile. "These young people need a break. How about if you and I go to your laboratory to run some tests?"

"I agree," smiled Nanchez.

~

Massive droning machines lined the cavern and warmed the production zone, a relief from the terminal chill emanating from the Dark Crystal to permeate the entire complex. Ponte and Nanchez moved through a gleaming metal lock at the far end of the section, down a winding passageway and through another hissing barrier, to enter the lab.

While the disarray in the Professor's workshop appeared to be the result of a minor hurricane, this space was tidy by comparison. Every tool was in its place and instruments lined a long workspace on the left. The right side was lined with panels that controlled the power produced by the Black Crystal and all the systems in the mountain. Tiny *orbs* and crystals blinked on and off and *messengers* displayed the functions of each machine.

"I understand how the system was controlled by changing the balancing crystal but how did you generate the power to form the storm?"

Nanchez smiled, "I created a filter that focused the power of the dark vectors. It was basically an amplifier but I didn't realize that I was tapping into another dimension, in spite of getting far more juice than I anticipated. I guess the question is whether we could use that filter to find the tangent points where the planes overlap?"

"It's a place to start," replied the Professor, as Nanchez opened a drawer and pulled out a black crystal on a silver chain.

"You'll be wanting this," he said, handing the priceless charm to the Professor and cranking up several instruments on the workbench. Two large *messengers* glowed, as the large man flipped switches and dialed in the settings. "I was focused on the island but I don't see why we couldn't expand that view, just as we did to monitor the movements of the Dark Forces."

One of the *messengers* displayed the island and the view slowly expanded to reveal the plane extending across the globe.

"Now let's see if we can use the filter that we developed to see the dimension they use for transportation," said Nanchez, as he fiddled with the settings on the second *messenger*.

A web of black vectors sizzled electric blue on the second screen. After an hour, the two men stood staring at the projected images floating above the workbench. In several places, a red glow indicated where the two planes overlapped.

"So they do touch," mused Ponte. "I might have suspected that they'd annihilate each other but we still don't know anything about the third plane...the one that they used to grab Adrian."

"And we don't know whether the Dark and the Light actually overlap. We'll need to combine the information from both systems, if we're going to reach a true understanding of these intersections. This could take a while."

Nanchez smiled, "But we do know that we can monitor their use of the Powers to control the weather and their movements along the vectors. If we can find the right frequency, we could monitor their communications!"

~

After Ponte and Nanchez careened away along the path to the mountain in the red trolley with the yellow fringe around the roof, the five *seers* and Ester gathered in the parlor. A sputtering fire hissed in the hearth and crackled in frustration, mirroring the mood in the room, after hours of rifling through endless hints and threads in the Books.

"I wish Adrian was with us," sighed Raffe, as he leaned his head back against the sofa and stared at the stars glimmering in the ceiling. "He'd see the solution."

"I miss him," moaned Alius. "Why don't we go see him?"

Everyone agreed and the five *seers* surrounded Ester. "We have no reason to believe that Zepallo is out there waiting for us," said Mary, "so I don't think you have anything to worry about."

"I'll put my faith in all of you." Ester grinned like a schoolgirl, "And I have to admit that I'm thoroughly jealous, every time you children leap into the vectors and soar off to someplace I can only imagine."

They zipped through the vectors and landed just outside the kitchen door at the House of Four Seasons.

Ester straightened her skirt, "That is so much fun."

The *seers* escorted her up the steps and into the kitchen, where Elsie and the twins were washing dishes and turned to greet their friends.

"How's it going at the observatory?" asked Megan, exchanging hugs.

"We think that we're making some progress," replied Mary. "The Professor and Nanchez are in the mountain trying to find the solution to a riddle in the dark planes."

"How's Adrian?" inquired Alius, quietly.

"There's been no change," replied Elsie, wiping a tear from her eye. "I can't convince Sara to take a break. She won't leave his side."

Ester wrapped Elsie in a hug, as the *seers* filed upstairs.

Sara looked up, as they entered Adrian's room, "I'm so glad to see you. Have you found anything new?"

The three young women walked over and hugged Adrian's mother. Simian and Raffe were a little bit hesitant to step through the doorway. "We think that we're making progress but I know, no matter how hard we try, it's not fast enough."

"How's Adrian?" asked Sky.

"He's the same as when you left," sighed Sara.

"I think you could use a rest," said Mary softly. "Why don't you take a break and we'll stay with Adrian for a little while."

Sara looked down at her son, "I sent Dr. Stevens home a couple of hours ago. He was exhausted and there really isn't much he can do here and I ordered John to bed, he's a wreck. The Doctor will be back in the morning."

"Go lie down for a few minutes and we'll come and wake you if anything changes. Ponte and Nanchez are at the mountain, so we can't really do much until we hear from them," said Alius. "Go on, we'll stay with Adrian."

Sara looked hesitant but she was so tired, her body listed from side to side. Mary picked up an *orb*, wrapped an arm around her waist, and guided her through the darkened hallway to her room.

Alius sat down on the edge of the bed and inspected Adrian's body. He was barely breathing. "I want to beat you up for being so stupid," she said softly, gently brushing blond hair off his forehead.

"He thought he could find the secrets of the Dark Forces," whispered Sky. "Even though he didn't know the dangers, it was a brave effort."

"We have to find a way to get him back," replied Alius, fighting tears overflowing her crystal blue eyes.

Sky walked over and rubbed her back, "We will. You just have to believe."

"I know and I do, but…"

The door creaked as Tic wandered into the room and hopped up on the bed next to Alius. "I was wondering where you were hiding!" smiled the little blond *seer*.

"I've been here since we first heard about all of this," said the black and white cat, brushing under Alius' chin. "I won't leave until you've found a solution and we have him back."

Sky rubbed the old tomcat's ears, "You've been involved in most of his adventures. Tell me about Adrian."

Tic sat down on the bed and stared at the boy, "The first time I met Adrian, my initial impression was that he was an immature, homesick child but I also sensed an inner strength…perhaps you might call it potential, and I suspected that he had the capacity to learn enough to become the *seer* to replace old Justus. When the storm came up and he first looked at the Book of Wisdoms, I knew he could become something more than just a *seer*. I told him that understanding would be demanding but there's no way I could have imagined it would be this challenging."

"What else?"

"When he volunteered to climb the mountain in the blizzard, I realized he had that special something extra…bravery. Then, when we organized the animals and the children to rescue Ester, I felt his empathy for the animals, his belief in the Balance of the natural world, and his concern for everyone's safety. We all gained great confidence from his manner and knew that his motivation was true and right. The animals adore him and there isn't anything we wouldn't do to help."

Sky and Alius looked at each other in a shared moment of inspiration, "I think we just might have another mission for you, if you're willing to help."

Tic looked up into Alius' eyes, "You know I'll do whatever you ask."

Sky smiled, "There's a dimension that is the world of animals. There are no humans but almost every species of animal that has ever lived is represented in this plane."

Tic stared at the tiny *seer* in disbelief, "A world without humans?"

"Yes."

"I would like to see this place," purred Tic.

"I'll take you there, when the time comes," smiled Sky. "We're not sure about how we'll get into Zepallo's den but when we've figured that out, we'll come for you."

"I'll be ready and I'm sure Brandy will want to come along too," said Tic, as he walked across Adrian's chest and licked his nose. "I want this one to turn back into the person he was. I miss him."

The door opened without comment and Mary stepped into the room, "Sara's asleep. She's exhausted."

"Good," replied Alius. "We can take turns sitting with Adrian until the Professor calls."

There was a quiet knock and Morgan appeared. "I don't mean to interrupt but I just had to know how he's doing."

Alius got up from the bed and walked over to hug her friend, "Please come in. We've just sent Sara to take a little rest. She hasn't slept since she found Adrian. Unfortunately, there's been no change in his condition but we think that we're making some progress."

Morgan walked over and stared down at Adrian's lifeless body. Tears dripped into his hair, as she leaned over to kiss his forehead. "Your bravery scares me," she whispered.

Alius walked up behind her to rub her back. "We all love him."

"I know," sniffed the tall girl. "I guess none of us realized how much we cared for him, until this happened."

Mary and Sky went down to the kitchen, leaving the two girls perched on either side of Adrian's bed. "Is there any hope?"

"We think we might be on to something but we won't know for a while. The Professor and Nanchez are working on some filters that might allow us to monitor the movements of the Dark Forces."

"I have faith in you."

Alius smiled, "Thank you but I honestly feel lost without Adrian's direction and insight. He always seemed to see through the chaos to the real solution to the problems that we've faced. Sky asked us about the character, the soul of Adrian. She thinks it might help to find a way to get him back. Tell me about the person that you knew…or know."

Morgan brushed the tears from her cheeks and stared at the pale face on the pillows wistfully. "I guess my first thought is the very first time I met him at the crescent beach, on his second day on the island. He was kind of shy and not really sure about what to expect on Morgan's Knot but I really liked him and tried to make him feel welcome. I know he was looking ahead to joining his parents in Vancouver and I got the feeling that he felt stuck here, until they were settled in their new home. That was before your battle on the mountain and rescuing Ester."

"My second memory happened on the way back from the Island of the Children. We were just within sight of the island and he was standing alone in the bow of the Jasmine. I walked up behind him and found that he was crying. I asked him what was troubling him and he said he wasn't sure whether he was worthy of the recognition that he'd received. He just wanted to be accepted as a normal boy, not a hero. I pointed out that he couldn't go back to being the person he was, when he arrived on the island. He'd matured into someone very special to all of us."

"We talked about it again, after all of you connected the nodes and he seemed more comfortable inside his own skin. He said that he only did what had to be done and any of us would have done the same things."

"That's something we all realized as we described him to Sky, he never took credit or did things for his own benefit. We joke that the *seers* are one for all and all for one...but he was the one. He guided us to the right course in every mission. The Professor felt the same way." Alius' smile faded, "Sky believes that he's the chosen *seer* who appears once in a thousand years. The one who can defeat the Dark Forces and lead us to the Light."

"I think she's right. There's something in his...being that touches everyone around him."

"Right," replied the blond *seer*, "and it's such a gentle, caring touch."

Morgan leaned across Adrian's body to hug Alius and they cried together.

~

The sun was cresting the eastern horizon, when George woke Alius, who was curled up on the foot of Adrian's bed. "Ponte's on the *messenger*," he said softly.

Alius looked around the room. Morgan was sound asleep, curled around Tic, on the other side of Adrian. Sky was sitting cross-legged, in deep meditation on the floor next to the bed. "Has Sara been asleep all night?"

"Yes," replied George with a gentle smile. "Thank you for coming. She needed a break."

Alius touched Sky gently and the tiny *seer* was instantly alert. "I think we're needed back at the observatory."

The two girls tiptoed downstairs to George's study, grinning at Raffe and Simian sprawled on the floor in the living room. Alius took a seat before the *messenger* and Ponte's impatient face. The gray hair fringing his shining dome was completely disheveled and his eyes were barely slivers, confirming an acute lack of sleep.

"Good morning, Professor."

"It is morning, isn't it," replied Ponte, turning to gaze out a window. "I think we've made some progress on this end. Could you come here?"

"Certainly, we'll see you in a few minutes," said Alius quietly.

"I assume that Ester is with you," mumbled the rumpled Professor. "How's Adrian?"

"He's the same. We stayed with him overnight, so Sara could get some sleep. She looked awful."

"I think I know how she feels," replied Ponte, removing his little glasses to rub an eye with a knuckle.

"We'll see you shortly," said Alius, flipping off the *messenger*. "Let's wake the boys and we'll leave Ester here. She can come back later."

Sky walked into the living room and roused the sleeping *seers*, while Alius slipped into the kitchen to tell George they were leaving. "We'll be in touch as soon as we know what's happening. The Professor says they've made some progress overnight, although he looks as if he hasn't slept in days."

"Thank you for coming," replied George, standing to hug Alius. "Mary's in our room. I'll wake her."

Moments later, he and Mary tiptoed down the stairs.

"The Professor called and asked us to meet them at the observatory. He seems to think they've found something," said Alius.

"Let's go!" whispered Mary.

The five *seers* walked out into the dawn. A cold steady gale rolled in off the ocean but the sky was clear and a tiny sliver of glowing orange was just peaking over the horizon. Simian smiled and stretched, "One for all and all for one!"

Everyone joined hands and moved off to the observatory.

Messengers lined every flat surface of the parlor and dining room and each was tuned to monitor a separate subject or frequency. The two Keepers wandered from one to another, talking in their strange language of fragments of the Keeper's dialect, which conveyed concepts and theorems, data and conclusions in mumbled gibberish. Their clothes were rumpled and Ponte's wild halo of hair swept out above the collar of his deep green waistcoat, as if he was facing into a mighty gale.

"Did either of you sleep?" inquired Alius.

"No, we were busy," snorted Nanchez.

"What is all this?" asked Sky, sweeping a hand across the *messengers*.

"Well, we've managed to find a few more things to monitor. This one shows the dark vectors," said Ponte, stifling a yawn, "and this one shows their energy plane. This one, on the dining room table, is monitoring their communications, although we haven't quite managed to reach a point where we can intercept their messages, we can see the traffic. That one, over there, shows the overlap of the dark dimensions. We're still working on a way to see where the positive and negative intersect but we've haven't quite got that one yet."

The *seers* wandered from one *messenger* to the next, "I wish we could hear their communications?" mused Raffe.

"We've been picking up normal traffic impulses but nothing that might indicate any significant movements."

Sky suddenly put her hand to her mouth, "I think I know how to find the overlaps!"

Chapter Five

George, Ester, Tic, and Brandy joined the group assembled in the parlor with an air of anticipation.

Sky's dark eyes were focused and the corners of her mouth barely curled into a perceptive grin, "Do you remember our conversation with Unis?"

The other *seers* nodded.

"Two thoughts suddenly gelled in my mind. The first was that the animals move between the planes to rescue endangered species. The second was that the animals of the night, the ones who fought alongside the Dark Forces, are confined to remote and isolated confinement."

Everyone stared curiously but no one responded.

"Don't you see, if the planes overlap, then we should be able to get into the dark planes through those places where the animals of the night have been exiled!"

Alius and Simian saw the inspiration instantly and jumped up to hug the tiny *seer*. A moment later, it dawned on the rest of the group and everyone started chattering.

Ponte and Nanchez were so tired that neither could quite grasp the revelation. They stood in the archway between the dining room and the parlor with their mouths agape, as the rest of the group jumped around in enlightened glee.

Finally, Ponte raised his hand for quiet, "I think I understand what you're saying but we'll have no way of monitoring your movements and, as far as we know, human beings were not designed to survive the energies of the dark planes."

Simian scratched his goatee, "Could you open a vector to that lake in the Caucasus Mountains?"

"Certainly," replied Nanchez.

"Then we could use that to get back," smiled the little Jamaican.

"We could paint it with positive vectors," laughed the Professor.

Raffe interrupted, "I wore that black pendant, while I was a captive in New York but I lost all control of my body, even if it did protect me from the energies of the Black Crystal and Zepallo's book."

"I wonder whether we could combine them with a positive crystal?" mused Nanchez.

"It's worth a try," smiled Ponte. "I've got enough golden crystals to supply everyone."

"I'm going to put out a call to some friends who can help. Could you supply couple of dozen, if needed?" asked Sky.

"Certainly," replied the Professor, as he wandered through the dining room and disappeared into the elevator. A few minutes later, he reappeared with a bag full of golden gems, "We have more than enough!"

Nanchez headed for the door, "I'll just make a run to the mountain for a matching set of black diamonds that are sitting on my workbench.

Sky smiled, "If you'll excuse me for a few minutes, I'll be back. I have to summon my friends."

She walked out through the front door, into a stubborn gale from the northeast, and settled on the cold ground, as Nanchez' utility truck rumbled along the path to the north. Her skin was barely warmed by the radiance of the sun, rising into a deep blue sky. She sensed the energy of a lone eagle hanging on the wind to the northeast. Although she learned to levitate when she was a young girl, she always marveled at the way birds used the air to move about in the atmosphere, suspended on a thermal or riding a wave of wind for hundreds of miles.

She quieted herself, moving into a deep meditation. *"I call to you Shambala, Master Chi, Lala, and Maze. We have devised a plan to enter the dark planes and I need your help. We will meet in the meadow of the unicorns in the plane of the animals. Everyone must wear a black crystal paired with a golden crystal, to protect us from the intensity of the dark energies, and we'll have extra stones, if needed. We'll need your knowledge, your powers, your weapons, and your friends. Please come quickly!"*

She rose and stared at twinkling sunlight glistening on the waves rolling across the ocean in nature's own perpetual rhythm. For the first time in days, she felt confident that they had discovered a path to finding the young *seer*, Adrian, and the foundation for the plan was born of his example.

Ester rummaged through her jewelry box to collect golden chains and returned to thread the links through the crystals before the fireplace, when Sky followed a blast of cold air into the parlor.

The auras in the room bristled with anticipation and purpose. Tic wandered over and rubbed against the tiny *seer's* leg, "I'm anxious to see this place you described but I'm even more eager to rescue our friend!"

Sky picked up the old cat and snuggled her nose into his soft fur, "I think you'll have an important role in this drama."

Ester placed a chain with two crystals around the necks of the five *seers* and gave each a kiss on the cheek. "I'll worry about you until you're all back in this room. What you are attempting is dangerous but I know that each of you will do your best to care for each other and for Adrian."

Sky hugged the slender woman. "I think we're all depending on the three of you to provide a path for our escape, once we've found Adrian. Just have the vectors ready."

Ponte smiled, "We'll begin as soon as you leave. The path will be there when you need it!"

George made no attempt to conceal his concern, "Just be careful. We've already got one *seer* in suspended animation and we don't want to lose anyone else!"

The five *seers* joined hands, as Sky instructed, "Let me guide you through the planes. I know where we're going. If any of you tries too hard, we'll fly off along the vectors and not reach our destination."

"Agreed," smiled the other four. Alius held Tic, who was sporting a red ribbon and twin crystals, and Raffe grasped a collar around Brandy's neck, adorned with another pair.

Everyone stared at the little woman, as she bowed her head and whispered an incantation that she learned as a young girl. A moment later they all disintegrated, leaving George, Ester, Ponte, and Nanchez staring in wonder at empty space.

"I wish we could do that!" sighed Ester.

Ponte smiled, "I'm just glad they can."

The five *seers* materialized on the edge of the meadow of the unicorns in the plane of the animals, followed by Shambala, Lala, and Maze. The tall African woman brought along a dozen slender young men and women, and more than a few who towered over her. They wore vibrant multi-colored robes, feathered headbands, and gold and silver bracelets that jangled on their wrists and ankles. A pendant, containing a golden crystal and a black crystal, was suspended from each of the *seers'* necks by intricately knotted lanyards.

Eight very small elderly people, who seemed incapable of stifling giggles and laughter, accompanied Lala and Maze. Curly white hair set off vivid amber eyes, blazing with an intensity that hinted at powers acquired through years of practice and perseverance, and each wielded a long staff with a glowing golden crystal on top and a pulsing black gem on the other end. The stout little *seers* wore heavy mountain clothing, pointed shoes that curled at the toe, and strange little hats listing precariously. The men all had frosty white beards and the women wore rings on most of their fingers, glittering with a variety of magical stones.

Sky hugged her friends and introduced everyone. The student *seers* from Africa bowed, their jewelry jingling with the sparkle of metallic raindrops. The elders from the mountains pursed their lips to make kissing sounds and then burst into peals of laughter, as they hugged anyone who happened to be near.

The herd of unicorns cantered across the meadow. Unis' horn glistened in the sunlight as she bowed to the *seers*, Tic, and Brandy. "We're honored to have you here."

Sky walked over to stroke her muzzle, "We're here on a mission and we need your help."

"You know that we would be happy to assist you in any way we can."

"Do you remember the young *seer*, Adrian?"

"Yes, I liked him," replied the beautiful unicorn, "a promising young *seer* glowing with potential." Her spiral horn was surely sculpted from the purest gold and her coat from driven snow.

"His spirit has been stolen by Zepallo and we're going to retrieve him. He's in the lair of the Dark Forces beneath a lake in the Caucasus Mountains."

"That is a dangerous undertaking," replied the unicorn.

"During our last visit, you mentioned two things that might allow for our success. The first was that you move between the planes to rescue the endangered species. The second was that there are places where the creatures of the night have been exiled. I'm hoping that the light and dark planes overlap in those areas."

"They do. That is why those creatures were banished to those places. We do not venture there and they are certainly not welcome here."

A wide-eyed Tic gazed around in wonder at this parallel world, "We've been on several missions with Adrian and some of these other *seers*. Brandy and I will accompany our friends alone, if need be, but we'd rather put together a massive legion of animals to invade the den of the Dark Forces. We've used that tactic as an overwhelming and indefensible diversion, which frees the *seers* to accomplish their goals."

Unis stared down at the black and white cat, "I must say that I admire your loyalty and dedication. We'll be happy to gather an army of animals to support you in pushing back the darkness."

"Now we're talking!" smiled Brandy.

Suddenly, the bright glow of Master Chi's aura materialized, accompanied by a small army of monks, clad in deep yellow robes. Each wore twin pendants of gold and black crystals on a chain of hand-hammered loops. "I'm sorry that it took so long to get here. Some of these youngsters are still wet behind the ears but they're willing and ready!"

Everyone cheered and marched along the path to the bluff overlooking the valley and gathered on a cliff and to marvel at the incredible diversity of animals roaming across endless grasslands that stretched away to a ring of green mountains cleft only by tributaries feeding a mighty river meandering off to the south.

A young bear, perched precariously on a rock in the rushing waters, thrashed for trout and salmon without much luck. His father sat on the bank making suggestions between fits of laughter. A lone eagle circled silently, hoping for an injured fish that he might swoop down to grab before the gullible bear could react.

Herds of animals from across the globe ambled from one meadow to the next, raising clouds of dust in their wake. Bison charged through topi, dikdik, and antelope, scattering the smaller animals from prized pasture.

A pride of lions stalked gazelle in the taller grasses, while cattle, sheep, zebra, wildebeest, and hartebeest watched with disinterest. In the distance, young elephants played in the shallows on the opposite side of the river from hippopotamus, water buffalo, and rhinoceros.

Flocks of birds in a rainbow of colors fluttered across the valley and enormous butterflies flitted through blazing ribbons of wildflowers growing at the base of the mountains. Along the bluff, the group could hear chipmunks and squirrels tittering, while raccoons peaked out from behind the trunks of the massive trees rising majestically into a dense canopy, camouflage for tiny monkeys peering down from branches high above.

Tic looked up at Brandy and blinked his eyes, "Is this heaven?"

The red setter leaned down and licked Tic's head, "I think this is as close as we'll get on this planet!"

The black and white cat purred, "I think you'll have to do the introductions. You can howl much louder than I can meow!"

Brandy slurped the top of the old cat's head again and raised his nose in the air, "I smell all sorts of friends." With that, he let out an uncharacteristic yowl that echoed across the plain.

Every animal in the valley turned to stare at the humans gathered on the cliff.

The *seers* moved down to an outcropping of rock, as animals streamed from the far reaches of the valley until the menagerie stretched for miles in every direction.

Mary leaned over to Alius and whispered, "This is giving me chills!"

"Me, too!" replied the blond *seer.*

Unis stepped to the edge of the cliff and bellowed, "My friends, our guests have come with a request for our help. A young *seer* has been kidnapped by the Dark Forces and, if you are willing, we're going to help to retrieve him."

"I'm sure that you've heard the stories about the connection of the nodes and the introduction of the animals to the humans in their meeting place. The young boy, who's been taken, is the *seer* who accomplished these feats. Although we live in this plane, we are all in his debt and our world is certainly in danger, if he is not rescued."

She bowed her head to Brandy and Tic, "You can't keep a secret in this world. Everyone knows everything about everyone!"

Turning back to the jostling herd stretching across the valley, she continued, "Those of you who wish to help, please move to the cut in the eastern mountains. We'll enter through the dark valley of the night creatures."

A mighty roar rose from the animals converged before the *seers.* There was no doubt about their intentions, as the churning mass slowly shuffled off across the valley.

Unis turned to the rest of the group, "We can't fly in there and it's a long walk, so we should get started. It will be evening before we reach the valley on the far side of the mountains."

The *seers* formed up in single column and followed the unicorns along a narrow path down through crags in the bluff and across the edge of the plain to begin the climb. Squirrels, mice, rats, chipmunks, raccoons, mountain lions, the little monkeys, and fluffy goats joined the parade, as the young Africans chanted a marching song. Their bracelets jangled as they walked, creating a pulsing percussion, which matched by the mountain people pounding their staffs on the rocks along the path in syncopated beats.

Hours later, an orange sun tickled the mountains to the west, illuminating a massive cloud of dust kicked up by the army of animals. The *seers* pushed through a narrow ravine that opened into a dark valley cleft between two mountains that crashed together in some ancient cataclysm. Steep rocky walls climbed to jagged peaks clawing into the deep blue sky and the few straggly plants and stunted trees clinging to the stones seemed to struggle for life.

The column stopped before a black pool and the unicorns and *seers* moved to the edge of the water. There was no evidence of night creatures.

Unis turned to Sky, "This is our entry point. Traveling along the dark vectors is much more difficult and uncomfortable than moving along the golden paths. You and Master Chi will have to guide us to our destination."

The tiny Thai *seer* turned to the old monk, "I know where we're going and I just realized how we can get into the lair of the Dark Forces. The Black Book told us that the lake is directly above the den, so it wouldn't surprise me to find that it's an entry point."

The chubby Master smiled, "The student of my student is teaching the Master!"

"We were given these black crystal pendants to protect against the dark energy and I'm glad to see that each of you has a similar pair," added Alius. "If the animals can cause enough commotion, we'll retrieve Adrian's spirit. As soon as we have him in our possession, everyone should gather around us to whisk him safely away. The Keepers of the

Powers on Morgan's Knot are going to paint the lake with positive vectors. We'll retreat along those paths."

The animals roared and the *seers* cheered.

Simian stepped forward, "Look at the aura that all of us are creating together. I believe that, if we move through this plane as one very large pool of energy, we'll be insulated from the negative powers that surround us."

All of the *seers* turned to look at the throng of animals crammed into the narrow valley and through the gap, where a tiny stream clawed a canyon through the mountain and glistened in the mighty golden glow illuminating the shadow world of the night creatures.

"No wonder we haven't seen any of the animals, who are supposed to live in this valley. To them it must seem like high noon!" laughed Raffe.

Master Chi raised his hands for silence and addressed the assemblage, "We believe that together, we form a massive energy. The plane that we will be entering is regulated by the Dark Powers and I would suggest that, as we move through this dimension in one continuous mass of light, we will protect one another!"

A deafening roar echoed up the valley, as the animals crowded closer together.

"Are we ready?"

"Yes!"

Alius wrapped her arms around Tic and Raffe grasped Brandy's collar. All of the *seers* stood at the edge of the pond and locked arms. The Africans, Master Chi's students, and the old people formed a second line ahead of the rowdy herd of animals, stomping, snorting, and howling in raucous anticipation. Sky looked up and down the chain of *seers* for assurance, before stepping into inky darkness.

Adrian felt his energy waning. He had no idea of how much time had passed, since falling hostage of this dark plane, but the glowing interior of the dark *orb* was sucking the essence from the vapor he had become.

He continued to sense murmurs and unintelligible comments from the dark *seers*. Occasionally, the *orb* felt as if it was being passed around, inspected, and thumped back on the table, amidst waves of aggression and frustration firing through the atmosphere of the Council Chamber.

Conjuring a vision of the other *seers* sitting around the table in the dining room at the observatory provided hope and he wondered what solution he might have found for this dilemma. His focus was drawn to the meadow where Unis and the unicorns grazed, knowing there was an answer to be found in their energy and wisdom and praying that his friends could find it without him.

Zepallo and the Council spent hours searching the texts for an answer to the quandary of the spirit in the black *orb*, sitting at the center of the table. With no obvious solution, tempers were fraying and alliances evaporating.

Ptolemy hissed, "This is a waste of time. We have other, more pressing duties that need our attention. Our plans and operations can not be delayed!"

Zepallo smiled, "My friend, those other matters are being attended to by competent professionals and the culmination is days away. We have the time. It is a question of persistence."

"I have no more patience for this endeavor," snarled Ptolemy, pushing his heavy chair away from the table to stand. "It's time for a vote. Do we continue with this nonsense or do we dispose of this…spirit, before it becomes a liability?"

There were murmurs among the group, each glancing back and forth between Ptolemy and Zepallo. This confrontation escalated into a matter of allegiance and yet another chapter in an ongoing power struggle within the Council of Ollapez. Several of the black-cloaked members stood, just as a courier appeared and whispered to Ptolemy.

He glared at Zepallo, "Our base is being painted with positive vectors! Do you know anything about this?"

"Do we know where these vectors originate?"

"Yes, we do," sneered Ptolemy. "They're emanating from the Golden Crystal on Morgan's Knot!"

"That's interesting," pondered Zepallo. "I might suggest that we send a pulse back along those paths. That should interfere with whatever technical wizardry they might employ!"

The courier looked back and forth between Zepallo and Ptolemy, unsure of whose instructions to follow. Finally, Ptolemy hissed, "Let it be done!"

The page ran from the chamber, as the divided Council continued jousting for authority and political position.

"We have not reached an agreement about this…this…spirit!"

"As a compromise, I might suggest that half the group return to their normal duties and the other half continue with our research. There is too much to gain from this opportunity and absolutely nothing to lose by continuing!"

Ptolemy looked sullen, "Agreed but, before anything else, you will attend to these wayward vectors personally." He turned and started for the door but stopped, as deafening alarms echoed through the complex. The members of the Council rose in panic and turned to Zepallo.

Ptolemy screamed, "What have you brought upon us?"

The whole complex shuddered as an enormous wave gushed from a breach in the lake above the lair, preceding a flood flowing through the tunnels, under the door, and across the chamber, washing over the boots of the Council Ministers. Screams echoed from the tunnels outside and Council members rushed to bar the door, only to be driven back by a surge of water blasting into the chamber.

Guards fought with very tall black people, yellow robed Orientals, and tiny white-haired geriatrics flying through the air, attacking the bewildered and unprepared troops, while a riot of animals scampered through swamped tunnels, overwhelming untested defenses. Ptolemy and several others heaved the shattered door closed, just as a panther and two lions leapt.

The Minister of the Interior screamed, "We're being invaded and there is only one person who bears the responsibility!" just as Alius, Sky, Master Chi, Shambala, Maze, Lala, Mary, Simian, and Raffe materialized on the opposite side of the room.

Mary, Raffe, and Simian aimed and fired blasts from Dadeus' rings to stun three of the Council members, foolish enough to raise their weapons, who fell into the torrent of water rushing across the chamber. Maze and Lala flew across the room to drop a golden net on another attempting to flee, while Shambala pirouetted gracefully and leveled two Council guards with an outstretched foot across the face. They crumpled to the floor.

Ptolemy and Zepallo both reached for the black *orb* at the center of the table but Zepallo was quicker. He grasped the *orb* and levitated to another exit on the opposite side of the room, only to find Tic, Brandy, Alius, Sky, and Master Chi barring his path.

The three *seers* hovered in front of the Dark Lord's only escape. "You'll not leave this room until we will have that *orb*!" shouted Alius, as Brandy snarled and grabbed the hem of his robes.

He stumbled across the room, struggling to dislodge the growling dog, and raised his hand to point his black diamond ring at the invaders.

Master Chi raised an outstretched palm, as a blast exploded from Zepallo's gem, gathered into a frizzling ball of blue lightning in front of the Master's hand, and turned back on its source. The charge slammed into the Dark Lord's chest, flipping him head over trumpets, and the *orb* flew up in an arc that brushed the ceiling. Sky flashed into a blur to catch the glowing black sphere before it hit the floor, "I've got him!"

The surviving members of the Council fled into the melee in the passage, leaving the chamber littered with moaning bodies. The *seers* gathered around the little Thai *seer* and moved to the door to the tunnels, where the defenders were being pushed back by an endless mass of warriors and comrades. Yellow-robed monks flew from one adversary to another, tall African *seers* smiled down at the guards, before hurling them through the channels, and old *seers* rode the shoulders of terrified troops, bashing them over the head and firing salvos of energy blasts from their diamond tipped staffs. With each surge flushing through the tunnels, the herd of unruly animals pushed the defenses farther and farther into the depths of the complex.

Panthers, lions, and tigers ambushed reinforcements attempting to enter the tunnel. Monkeys scampered across the piping overhead, while smaller animals scurried through the onslaught, gnawing on anything that might prove useful to the Dark Forces, scrambling up the legs and uniforms of the guards to bite any exposed flesh. Alligators sloshed through the gushing river flowing through every level, snarling and snapping at petrified guards. A giraffe leaned low to intimidate one dark warrior with huge dark eyes and a slurpy black tongue, as it launched another with its hind feet, while an ape hurled soldiers to splatter through the deluge. Large bears swung mighty paws and clouds of bees, wasps, hornets, and mosquitoes swarmed. Camels lumbered through the tussle, carting dozens of smaller cats on their backs, as packs of dogs, fox, and coyotes charged through the chaos.

Tic and Brandy sat in the doorway, watching the battle tumbling through the concourse. "This looks like fun!" exclaimed Brandy, bounding into the scuffle.

The black *orbs* in the ceiling flickered on and off, generating an eerie purple strobe pulsing the clamor into flashing frames of an old horror film. A deafening sound of human screams and the roar of the animals reached a crescendo when a pair of elephants crashed through a steel barrier, driving a hundred guards back along the corridor. They were followed by an immense herd of bison, antelope, water buffalo, wildebeest, deer, elk, moose, horses, and zebras charging through the passageways. Tic leapt onto the back of a passing buffalo, as it hurtled along the tunnel with the throng, which was flowing in a massive wave of creatures to fill every space in the complex.

Alius wondered whether the last of the animals had even reached this dark world. The *seers*, emerging from the Master's chamber, were sucked along by the tide of animals, until they reached an immense dome carved into bedrock. Giant screens lined the walls and hundreds of spherical workstations floated around a central podium.

The animals charged through the enormous space, knocking everything and everyone out of their path to secure the six entrances. Squads of guards tried to enter the cavern from three steel locks on the opposite wall but they were no match for the animals, who pushed them back down the channels. Banks of equipment exploded, sparks cascading in beautiful showers of red and yellow, blue and magenta. Hawks and eagles tore at the screens as they swept through the cave, flocks of birds swirled around the ceiling, and the central podium collapsed when several *seers* levitated a pair of hippopotami to the balcony surrounding the pod.

Total chaos seemed to be under control, as Alius turned to Sky, who was cradling the black *orb* inside her robes.

"Now all we have to do is figure out how to get him out of here!" shouted Alius.

"I think we'd best leave that to Master Chi," replied Sky, glancing at the *orb*. "Our mission is accomplished. We should take Adrian back where he belongs!"

Simian put his fingers in his mouth and whistled. The commotion around them ceased for an instant. "We've got what we came for. Finish what you're doing and let's get out of here!"

The control center shuddered under a collective groan of disappointment, as the other *seers* and animals were having too much fun overwhelming the Dark Forces and seemed reluctant to end the carnage.

Unis trotted up to the *seers*, "We could cause a lot more damage to their facilities, if you'd give us a few more minutes!"

Alius and Sky grinned, "Don't let us spoil your fun but we just want to be sure that all of our friends get away safely."

"I'll make sure that everyone gets out," smiled the beautiful unicorn. "Other than saving endangered species, we don't get to make a difference in your world very often. It's the least we can do!"

"We can't lose sight of our goal," responded Sky. "We have to get this *orb* to safety."

"Then go ahead. We'll follow your path, as soon as we've finished our task."

Sky and Alius hugged the beautiful unicorn, "Be safe!"

Unis bowed to her friends, "You get Adrian's spirit back where it belongs. We'll see you shortly!"

The *seers* clustered around Alius, Sky, and the *orb*, a shield against the surreal pandemonium churning through the cavern. A moment later, they vanished.

Chapter Six

Ponte, Ester, Nanchez, and George had been monitoring the *messengers* since moments after the *seers* left the parlor, afraid to leave the room, in case something happened that might hint at the progress of an invasion they could not monitor.

A small beep escaped the *messenger* monitoring the dark vectors through Nanchez' filter. The four leapt from their seats to huddle in the glow. The red dot over the Black Crystal in the Caucasus Mountains was pulsing.

Ponte leaned back, staring at the flashing speck on the screen, "They've disrupted the circuits of that Black Crystal!"

Ester covered her mouth and whispered, "I wish we could see what's happening."

"I'm afraid we'll have to wait to hear this tale," smiled George, "but that's a good sign."

"Let's check the vectors we put in place," yawned Nanchez, shuffling to the next *messenger* to find a blip whizzing across the globe towards Morgan's Knot.

"They're on their way home!" laughed Ponte.

Frozen in place for a moment, staring at the dot racing through the floating image, they rushed out the front door into the frosty morning. The sun was just peeking over the horizon and an orange glow fringed puffy clouds sweeping across the ocean.

In rapid succession, a strange assortment of unusual characters materialized on the lawn in front of the observatory. Very tall Africans and yellow-robed Asians intermixed with small people, with white hair and strange little hats that tilted to one side or the other, who giggled incessantly, surrounded the *seers*.

The Africans chanted in deep rhythmic tones, their bracelets and anklets jangling in a hypnotic beat. The small people pounded long staffs on the frozen ground and the yellow-robed monks twirled around in dizzying spirals.

Slowly, the group parted and Sky handed the *orb* to Alius, who walked up to the adults standing on the front stoop, "Adrian is inside this black *orb*. We hope our friend, Master Chi, will be able to free him."

Ester rushed to hug her young charge, "I'm so glad that all of you are home safe!"

Sky introduced Master Chi, Maze, Lala, and Shambala. Everyone shook hands and Ponte escorted the throng into the house. They enjoyed entertaining but the observatory had never accommodated so many bodies.

Each of the new guests stopped and gazed around the parlor, marveling at the stars glowing in the ceiling above two stories of books, historic treasures, and scientific curiosities, including the tiny glowing *orbs* orbiting in the model of the Solar System and a rattling skeleton in the corner. Alius placed the *orb* on the dining room table and turned to Master Chi. "Can you free him?"

"I think that we can find a solution to this problem, my dear," smiled the chubby old *seer*. "Where is Adrian's body?"

"He's in another house, not far from here," replied Ester.

"How is he?" asked Raffe.

"He's the same as he was when you left," said George quietly.

"Then let us consult the texts to be sure of the progression that we should follow," smiled Master Chi, spinning the black *orb* in his hands.

Alius placed the Book of Wisdoms on the table and the room fell silent, as all of the guests crowded in to hear the reading.

Master Chi sat in the chair usually occupied by Adrian, set the *orb* in the middle of the table, and opened the heavy cover of the golden book. Simian stood behind him while Raffe, Mary, Sky, and Alius took chairs and leaned close.

"The spirit of a young *seer* is captive in this black *orb*. We wish to free him and return his essence to his body."

"This is a dangerous operation."

"Can it be done?"

"Yes."

"And how would we accomplish this task?"

The figures in the Book rushed around the pages for more than a minute. Finally, they stopped and formed a golden diamond. "The vectors of the Golden Crystal must be directed to the victim's body. When they are focused, the *orb* must be opened inside the Golden Crystal. The spirit will flow through the vectors to be deposited in his body. Any fluctuations in the power of the vectors will redirect his energy and disperse it throughout the planes."

Master Chi smiled at Alius, who was sitting directly across the table, and closed the book. "I feel confident that we can return Adrian's spirit to his body."

He turned to Ponte and Nanchez, "I noticed the *messengers* that you've been using to monitor our movements. I must assume that you are the Keepers of the Powers?"

Ponte and Nanchez grinned, "At your service!"

"Could you direct the positive vectors to the house of our young friend?"

"It might take a little finagling but, yes, we can!" laughed Ponte. "If you'll follow me, we'll begin."

Alius picked up the black *orb* and followed the group to the elevator. The *seers* packed into the tiny car and descended to the white room, before turning down the hallway into the Professor's workshop. Small groups of guests packed into the tiny elevator and massed against the curved walls around the blazing Golden Crystal.

The Professor and Nanchez darted back and forth along the workbench, collecting tools and connectors. Ponte lit up a *messenger*, as Nanchez flipped switches and stretched wires from one instrument to another, until a tangle of multicolored connections covered the whole surface.

Ponte stared impatiently at the *messenger*, as the links formed in sequence. Slowly, the glowing arcs of the golden vectors shifted to focus on the House of the Four Seasons. The Professor beamed, "I believe we have the energies all lined up."

Sky looked worried, "We'll have to be quick. Our animal friends will need the vectors, that you focused on the lair of the Dark Forces, to escape. They're depending on us!"

"Then we must hurry!" said Master Chi.

Everyone trooped out of the workshop and down the hallway into the white room, where they found all of their comrades standing silently in a circle in the blinding glow of the Golden Crystal.

Alius offered the *orb* to Master Chi, "I think that you should be the one to release his spirit. I want to be with him when he returns to his body."

Master Chi accepted the *orb* and smiled at the little *seer*, "I understand completely and I will do my best to follow our instructions precisely. If you are going to be there, you should leave now."

Alius hugged the old man and turned to her friends, "Thank you, all of you." With a small knowing smile, she bowed her head and disappeared.

Ponte leaned down and brushed the gold dust away from the slot in the floor. He pulled a key from the pocket of his rumpled waistcoat and inserted it.

A loud, booming voice asked, "Who seeks entry?"

All of the *seers* in the room covered their ears, as Master Chi stepped up to the spinning Crystal and replied, "I am Master Chi. I am a *seer!*"

The rotation of the giant gem increased dramatically and a dark shadow washed down the side. Master Chi held the *orb* reverently, close to his body, and stepped inside.

The breach closed behind him and he was surrounded by the marching figures from the Book of Wisdoms. Slowly, they moved away to reveal the spinning globe of the earth. The huge landmass of Pangaea split apart and the continents swept into their current positions. The large voice asked, "How may We help you?"

"I have the spirit of the young *seer*, Adrian, inside this black *orb*. The Books instructed me to focus the vectors on the house that holds his body and, by releasing this essence inside the Crystal, he would be returned to his normal state."

"We have been aware of the disturbance of his absence. His spirit is very strong but his energies are faint."

"How would I open this *orb*?"

The voice was silent for a moment, "We sense that the vectors are stable, so it is safe to begin this operation. The *orb* will open by twisting the top and bottom in opposite directions. The top must be turned to the east, the bottom to the west."

"There is one more thing that I must ask, before we begin."

"We are listening!"

"When we have completed this task, the vectors must be returned to their previous positions to allow for the escape of our animal allies from the lake in the Caucasus Mountains."

"We will see that it is done."

"Thank you," smiled the Master, as he grasped the *orb* and twisted it as instructed. A pale gasping sound, as air rushed into the *orb*, preceded a beautiful golden wisp escaping to float like tiny tornado at the very center of the Golden Crystal, undisturbed by a howling wind roaring around the inside of the spinning stone. The vapor pulsing with life, swirled into a glowing sphere and disappeared in a blinding flash.

Alius materialized on the walkway below the kitchen door. *"I hope this works!"* she thought, marching up the steps.

Elsie and the twins were busy in the kitchen, preparing breakfast, and rushed to hug Alius.

"What's happening?" asked Megan.

The little *seer* smiled, "We retrieved Adrian's spirit. It was being held in a black *orb*. I think that he'll be returned to his body in the next few minutes!"

Molly and Megan hugged the little *seer* and squealed with delight. Alius rushed up the stairs to the second floor with Elsie and the girls in tow and John close behind.

They found Sara and Morgan, sitting in chairs next to Adrian's bed and Sara was bent over resting her forehead on the blanket next to her son. Alius walked over and rubbed her shoulders gently.

Sara turned with a start and stared up at the blond *seer*. "You're back," she said softly, her cheeks stained with tears, her eyes gray with exhaustion and anguish.

"And so is Adrian," smiled Alius, glancing over at her friend, who twitched and coughed several times before his eyes fluttered.

Numbed by days of worry, Sara stared at Adrian and then back to Alius with disbelief, before she reached out to brush her son's hair out of his face and leaned to kiss him, "Welcome back."

Adrian looked up at his mother and smiled.

Dr. Stevens arrived, moments after the boy regained consciousness. He checked his pulse, listened to his heart, took his temperature, and looked into his eyes. "You are a lucky young man. How do you feel?"

"Weak," whispered Adrian, "and thankful."

"You have your friends to thank for your salvation, I'm afraid I couldn't do much more than keep your body hydrated with healing waters."

Adrian smirked, "Thanks, it would have been horrible to get rescued, only find that I didn't have a body to come back to."

The Doctor turned to Sara, "Keep him in bed for a few days and let's see whether he regains his strength. We have no way of knowing what complications might arise from all of this because I'm fairly sure it's never happened before. I'll be back this evening."

"Thank you for coming," said Adrian's mother, hugging the doctor.

As he was about to leave, Kelly ran into the room, "You've got to come and see this!"

Adrian started to sit up and collapsed back into his pillows.

"You stay put," insisted his mother, as she straightened his blankets. "I'll stay with you."

Everyone else trooped out of the room and down the stairs. Kelly led the parade out through the front door and stopped on the steps, staring in awe at the incredible herd of animals stretching for as far as the eye could see in every direction.

The *seers*, monks, warriors, and old people materialized on the lawn with George, Ester, Ponte, and Nanchez, just as Unis pushed to the front to stand at the bottom of the steps.

"How is Adrian?" she asked, as she bowed slightly, her golden horn glistening in brilliant sunshine.

Dr. Stevens looked down at the beautiful creature. "He's regained consciousness and I think we should be thanking all of you!"

"Adrian holds the potential to salvage the future of your world. We do not venture into this plane unless there is a species close to extinction but, in this case, dealing a blow to the darkness was the least we could do."

Alius looked concerned, "Did all of our friends escape safely?"

"We made sure that all of our allies had evacuated the lair. I would say that our efforts were most successful!"

A cheer went up from the humans, followed by a deafening roar from all of the animals.

"I'm afraid that we will have to take our leave. It is time for us to return to our world but all of you are welcome to visit," smiled Unis.

Alius and Sky hugged the beautiful unicorn, as Tic and Brandy rubbed against her legs.

"Thank you," said Sky quietly, "I'm in your debt."

"You owe us nothing, my dear. If your world is destroyed, so is ours. Think of this mission as self-defense to protect the Power of the Light that guides us all! You know where to find us, if we can help in the future."

Unis turned to the other animals, "It's time for us to return to our plane."

A moment later, a river of animals charged around the barn and up the ridge, where they disappeared into the vent, leaving no trace other than a cloud of dust and a trail of matted grasses.

Kelly looked up at Dr. Stevens, "No one will believe this!"

The Doctor looked down at her wonderful smile, "I think they represent everything that our world might be someday."

Kelly laughed, "I sure would like to go visit them!"

~

Adrian felt weak, as he rolled over to stare out the window at sunshine lighting up rippling wheat in fields to the east. His mother, Elsie, Molly, Megan, Morgan, and Alius took turns making sure that he stayed down, until Dr. Stevens decided he was strong enough to get out of bed.

Adrian secretly began calling them 'the ladies' auxiliary' but he did not protest and welcomed their care. His father and George slipped in, occasionally, to talk for a few minutes, only to be shooed out of the bedroom by one of the ladies.

It felt so good to be back inside his own body and he realized how each of us takes our lives for granted. We accept good health as normal and inexhaustible but being separated from his body provided a perplexing perspective, that resulted in appreciating every moment of life as precious.

Morgan sat quietly in a chair beside the bed, staring at him. Their eyes met and she said, "I don't know whether to be mad at you or just glad that you're back with us!"

Adrian blushed, "I'm sorry I scared everyone. It's funny, well not really, but as a captive inside that *orb*, I was thinking about all of you…the things we've done together, things each person said to me. Words that touched me and seemed so much more…I don't know, relevant to what was happening. I kept hoping that all of you would find a way to bring me back."

"I think you have Sky and Alius to thank for that. Actually, there was a small army of *seers* who helped. Master Chi, an old Thai *seer* who taught Sky's mentor, brought more than a dozen monks. An African woman, Shambala, brought another couple of dozen very tall warriors, and an older couple, Maze and Lala, showed up with a bunch of tiny old people who couldn't stop laughing all the time. Then there were the animals…"

"The animals?" inquired Adrian, with a quizzical look.

"Yes," smiled Morgan. "You missed all the fun. Remember the menagerie you put together to rescue Ester?"

"Sure."

"Well, multiply that by a hundred or, maybe a thousand, and include every animal you can imagine and you might just be approaching the herd that showed up on the island, after they rescued you!"

"You're kidding?"

"No. I think Sky brought the animals."

"Was there a unicorn?"

"Yes, a whole herd of them. They were so beautiful and seemed so kind and gentle but I was also aware that they were definitely in charge," giggled Morgan. "I'm still not sure I believe they exist!"

"The animals from the plane," murmured Adrian.

"They filled the yard and every path leading north and south for as far as the eye could see. It was amazing."

"I'm sorry I missed them. Their plane is a very special place."

"Unis said that if you ever need their help again, just let her know."

"I know we'll need their help again," said Adrian quietly. "I don't think this is over."

Morgan's grin wilted, "What are you saying?"

"I'm still kind of fuzzy but I honestly feel that the Dark Forces will want revenge for the mess we made of their plans. While I was in their lair, I kept feeling they were moving rapidly towards something that could change the balance of the world."

"You're frightening me," whispered the tall girl.

"I'm frightening myself," responded Adrian, swinging his legs over the side of the bed. "I have to talk with Ponte."

"You're not supposed to get up!"

"I know but this might be important!"

"What if I have him come here?"

"Is Alius here?"

"Yes, she's downstairs."

"Okay, I'll compromise," said Adrian. "Would you ask her to come up?"

"Sure, I'll be right back," replied Morgan, pushing him into his pillows and kissing him on the cheek.

Adrian looked up, thinking, *I'm glad that you're my friend. Maybe someday, I'll be taller than you...or maybe not.*

Within moments, Alius knocked on the old door, which opened with a cheery, "Please come in."

Adrian was barely upright, dangling his legs over the edge, and feeling a bit dizzy. Alius sat down in the chair facing the bed and Morgan walked in behind her. "We need to talk with the Professor. I have a strange feeling that the Dark Forces will want revenge for what you did to their facilities and their plans."

"Do you really think they might attack Morgan's Knot?"

"We're the only ones who stand in their way. Eliminate us and their plans suddenly become less complicated," replied Adrian, falling back on his elbows. "That time I took my mother along the vectors to visit our old house, we ran into Zepallo and he showed us a vision of a huge fire raging across Morgan's Knot. At the time, I thought it was just a cruel concoction to scare us but, considering everything that's happened, I'm not so sure anymore. While I was in that dark plane, I saw the Crystals on the island and the Island of the Children exploding, the major cities of the world abandoned and destroyed, hurricanes, tornadoes, and floods across the globe."

"I'll call the Professor," said the little *seer*, rising to leave. She turned back to Adrian, "I hope you're wrong."

"I hope I am too."

~

Ptolemy, Zepallo, and the other Dark Masters toured the remnants of the control center beneath the lake. Most of the sentries overseeing the excavation wore bandages and slings and more than a few shuffled along with the aid of crutches.

The deluge had been plugged and millions of gallons of water pumped from the tunnels but the equipment in the dome was in a shambles. Fortunately, the animals could not breach the core protecting the Black Crystal, so the power source remained intact, but they shorted out most of the control circuits.

"Lightning in a bottle?" screamed Ptolemy. "I would suggest that, once again, you've misjudged the power of your young *seer* and his friends. This will set us back months!"

Zepallo did not respond, deep in thought, remembering the destruction to the lairs beneath Ice Island and Central Park. *"How could this gifted child cause so much chaos and devastation to our facilities and my plans? He's only just moved to a sleepy, though magical, island in the North Atlantic, where the primary focus is farming. He's been shielded from the Powers through his childhood on the mainland, and, certainly, has not endured years studying the texts, learning from the Masters, or slowly earning his place through any hierarchy, although I'm sure Professor Ponte is a fine tutor."*

The Dark Lord passed up several opportunities to kill the young *seer*, with the hope that he might tempt him into the fold, but Adrian's persistence and power disrupted their campaign and nothing could be allowed to impede his march to final triumph.

The young *seer* was an embarrassment to Zepallo's tottering stature and, ultimately, his power. Ptolemy and the other Masters were merely pawns in his plans to rule the world. He manipulated them, guided them to make favorable decisions and wield the power of the Council to unite the Dark Forces behind a carefully crafted strategy to overwhelm the World Powers from within. Their surrogates would guide the authorities, controlling governments, militaries, financial markets, religious institutions, and communications, to the brink of self-destruction. Amidst roiling panic, they would convince the world population that the savior, Zepallo, and only Zepallo, could tame the chaos and bring order to a planet gone mad.

No, this young *seer* must be dealt with swiftly and decisively. Nothing could be allowed to stand between the Dark Lord and his ultimate quest, especially a most exceptional and annoying child.

Ponte and Nanchez took chairs facing Adrian's bed. Alius reached to prop up her friend, who was wilting into his pillows. He looked terrible and she was afraid that it might be a long time before he regained his strength or his determined spirit.

"How are you feeling?" inquired Ponte, gently.

"I'll be alright when I get some energy back," replied Adrian.

"Alius tells us that you are concerned about the Dark Forces."

"That's true," said the young *seer*, quietly, struggling to sit up straighter. "I've been thinking about the time I spent in their lair. It wasn't that I could actually understand what was going on, it was more a feeling that they were moving towards a final solution to control the world. We've managed to disrupt their plans twice before and I have to wonder how long they'll allow us to interfere before they react."

"I see your point," muttered Nanchez, glancing at the Professor. "We really have no defenses in place, if they decide to invade the island."

"True," sighed the old man, looking over his glasses at the young *seer*, who was swaying slowly from side to side. "We do have systems to scan the horizon and filters that are monitoring the dark vectors but...basically, you are correct. We have no defense against an invasion."

"So, we're in the same position that you were in, when our guards kidnapped Ester?" inquired Alius.

Ponte was slow to reply, "Once the imminent threat was eliminated, there seemed no pressure to construct a real defensive strategy, so you are infuriatingly correct."

Adrian was looking pale and seemed destined to topple over to one side or the other, "I know my thoughts might seem paranoid and I hope, I truly hope, that I'm wrong...but what if I'm right?"

The two Keepers stared at the boy, accepting the logic and reasoning behind his insight, "Let us look into what systems might be put in place and we'll get back to you in a little while."

"Fine," replied the young *seer* as he rolled across the mattress, "someone should warn the Island of the Children, Simian...and Sky and her friends..."

Alius heaved Adrian's legs under the covers and tucked him in with a kiss on his forehead. She turned to the two men, looking disturbed and concerned, "You know he's right. If Zepallo decides to eliminate Adrian, his path to becoming king of the world would be clear."

The Keepers had witnessed enough examples of the Dark Lord's appetite for violent expediency to recognize that he would not hesitate to destroy the island in his quest to eliminate his young foe. The hurricane that approached Jamaica proved his complete disdain for human life. The absence of Adrian's spirit made them all aware of how much they depended on the boy, his insights, and his bravery. The young *seer* only arrived on the island last summer and, now, he represented everything that their society had built over generations.

"Let's return to the observatory to see what we can come up with," whispered the Professor. "I'll contact Dadeus to warn them and seek his advice. You get in touch with Simian and Sky. We might also consider finding a way to hide our young *seer*, in case of an invasion."

Alius turned to look down at her sleeping friend, "Agreed. He might be delirious but he also might be right."

Chapter Seven

The blond *seer* landed on a beach on the northern coast of Jamaica and was instantly consumed by a warm soggy breeze blowing in from the ocean. She pulled off her jacket, kicked off her shoes, and pranced up the winding stairway until she found a cluster of thatched cottages, nestled in a protective nook in the hillside and surrounded by voluptuous gardens.

She spied an older woman, harvesting breadfruit and depositing her bounty in a large wicker basket, who turned to face the young *seer* with a broad grin, "We don't get many tiny, pale, white-haired tourists in our little village. You must be Alius! I've heard much about you!"

The little *seer* blushed, "I'm afraid I don't know your name."

"Simian does not willingly share information. Coaxing doesn't work, you have to pry it out of him." The old woman laughed, "I'm his wife, Lorraine."

"I'm very pleased to meet you," replied the little *seer*.

"Come along, let's sit in the shade, where it is a little cooler," said Simian's wife, leading Alius to a bench beneath a large banyan tree. Crooked branches swept down to brush damp earth and air-roots, interwoven into lacey dangling tongues, formed a living curtain around them. The old woman poured orange juice from a metal pitcher into two glasses and offered one to her guest.

"Is Simian around?"

"He's at the market. He's been gone so much, lately, our income from the sale of our fabrics is down. He should be back in an hour or so. Is there anything that I could help you with?"

"No, I need to talk with him. We fear the Dark Forces might want retribution for the destruction of their facilities and disrupting their plans."

"Simian told me about your latest mission. I loved the part about the animals, that must have been an amazing herd you put together."

"It was so huge that I really don't have any words that are adequate to describe it," smiled Alius, "other than, I think the battle was won long before the last of them arrived in the cavern beneath the lake. They completely overwhelmed the Dark Forces and destroyed the facility."

"I can see your point about the possibility of revenge. This is the third time that you've frustrated their plans."

"True, but all of our efforts have centered around Adrian, because he brought the Forces of the Light together. Eliminating him would change the balance."

"How is the young *seer*?"

"The doctor thinks that he'll recover but he's weak and delirious at the moment."

"My husband has great respect, not only, for his powers but for his strength of character. He spoke about the meeting you had with the Thai *seer*, Sky, that each of you offered different perspectives. Yet everyone agreed that Adrian is probably the one *seer*, who comes along in many lifetimes, who might have the power to push back the Darkness."

Alius smiled, remembering the conversation, "I don't think any of us really stopped to think about his influence or the gentle way he guides each of us to reach beyond anything that we've done before."

"From what Simian's told me, he doesn't know how important his contribution has been," said Lorraine quietly. "True leaders are like that."

Alius stared into the old woman's dark eyes, tired but calm and overflowing with the joy of life. "You're married to one of them."

Simian's wife laughed and laughed before she said, "That's true but you, as a young lady, must learn that no man is ever complete without a strong woman to guide him along his path. Simian was a rascal when I met him. It's taken years of training to turn him into the man that he is today but, in spite of all my efforts, he's still a rascal!"

Alius laughed, "I'll remember that!"

Just then, Simian stuck his head through the screen of air-roots hanging from the old tree and grinned at the two women. "I'd guess that you've introduced yourselves!"

Lorraine poured another glass of juice for her husband, as he sat cross-legged on a gnarl of tangled roots, "I'm afraid to ask why you're here?"

"Adrian's starting to come around and he suggested that the Dark Forces might seek revenge, after our third success in trashing their facilities. He thinks the next logical step is to eliminate him. After all, he's the one who brought the Forces of Light together and he's the one who stood up to Zepallo. I hate to admit that I think he might be right."

Simian stroked his gray goatee and stared at the blond *seer* over the rims of his little glasses. "It will take them a while to recover from the destruction of the lair beneath the lake but I agree with your suspicions. What do Ponte and Nanchez think?"

"They're looking into the possibility of building a defense and they're contacting Dadeus, Mary, and Raffe on the Island of the Children. I'm assigned to talk to you and then find Sky."

"We have no way of knowing their plans but an invasion by their forces would be hard to defend. Have you considered taking him off the island?"

"No," replied Alius. "We're not that far along with a plan. At this point, it's merely a suspicion and, besides, Zepallo wouldn't hesitate to destroy the island in his quest to get to Adrian. I'm not sure that he'd be safe anyplace on the planet."

"What if he was not on the planet?"

"The planes! We could hide him in the planes and they'd never find him. On the other hand, they might demolish the island anyway and I'm sure the Evil One's systems monitor the positive vectors. That's how he intercepted Raffe and Mary."

"And you wouldn't have Adrian to help in this battle," injected Lorraine. "No, this is a fight that needs to be fought straight on. Win this one and you can drive them back into hiding for years to come!"

The two *seers* stared at the old woman, until Simian finally smiled, "Why are you always right?"

"Because I have to be smarter than you are, just to keep up!"

~

Alius landed on a narrow path winding through lush jungle, beneath layers of trees rising into a dense canopy, filtering shafts of brilliant sunlight to flaunt a profusion of flowers blooming in incredible colors.

She looked up and down the trail, opening her senses to the energies, and started climbing the hill to the north. Around a turn, she found two young boys playing on boulders in a gushing stream that etched the jagged canyon through sheer rock. Their yellow robes were sopping wet and their shaven heads glistened in the morning light, but their laughter faded, on finding a pallid girl with white hair standing on the bank above them.

Alius smiled, which seemed to calm their fears, and they scrambled up the rocks to greet her. "I'm looking for Sky."

The two boys laughed and grabbed her hands, dragging her along the trail. Birds swooped above their heads and clouds of butterflies, in a rainbow of hues and patterns, flitted from one bloom to the next. They crossed a little bridge over the stream, where the track zigzagged up through the face of the gorge. At the top, they came to a pool surrounding a magnificent temple rising above a tiny village tucked into the forest. Sky stood alone on the steps and Alius could sense that she was expecting them.

The two boys ran across the water. Alius watched them and wondered whether there were stepping stones hidden just beneath the surface, although she could not see anything in the dark water.

Sky laughed and called to her friend, "You just have to believe!"

Alius was hesitant. She could levitate herself to the tiny *seer* but that seemed like cheating. If the two young boys could make this crossing, then so could she. She took a deep breath and stepped off the edge, staring straight at Sky.

"Don't look at your feet, they know where they're going. Look at me. See yourself beside me!"

Alius took tentative steps until, gradually, she gained confidence and marched across the pond.

The tiny Thai *seer* greeted her friend with a big hug, "Welcome to the Temple of Spiritual Harmony. I sensed that you were near. I hope you're not bearing bad news."

Alius smiled, "I don't know whether the information I carry is bad…yet, but I could use your advice and, perhaps, your help."

Sky took her arm, "Come along, we'll have some tea."

They followed a path of smooth black pebbles around the temple and Alius could hear the low rumble of many people chanting, the tinkling of little bells, and an overwhelming scent of sweet incense. Sky led her through a voluptuous garden to a very simple structure comprised of four posts bearing a roof of blue tiles curving into a peak at the top. Long planks of smoothed and polished bamboo formed a seamless floor reflecting gleaming light spilling through the foliage.

The two boys followed along and, after the young women settled on large pillows, produced a silver tray with a small teapot, two delicate china cups, and a tiny bowl of brown sugar. They bowed, backed out of the pavilion, and disappeared.

Sky poured green tea into two tiny cups and offered one to Alius. "How can I help you?"

The blond *seer* sipped her tea before saying, "Adrian is coming around. He's still weak but we think he'll recover. He's concerned that the Dark Forces will attempt an attack on the island, first, in retribution for the destruction of three of their facilities and, second, to eliminate the threat he poses."

Sky was silent, for a long moment, as she stared at her friend, "His conclusion does not surprise me. What else did he say?"

"While he was captive in their lair, he got the feeling they were moving towards completing preparations for something big. We all know that Zepallo and his comrades want to rule the world but Adrian and the rest of us stand in their path. Whatever they're planning would be much easier, if they could eliminate him at the outset."

There was no smile in Sky's eyes, "Have you considered moving him to someplace safer?"

"We haven't really developed a plan but we're sure that Zepallo would not hesitate to destroy the island, if he thought he could kill Adrian."

"He'd probably destroy the island anyway and move on to the Island of the Children, just to be sure."

"You're beginning to see why I'm concerned."

"All of this is based on Adrian's feelings or suspicions?"

"Yes, he might be delirious but it does make sense."

"I agree," pondered the tiny *seer*. Long dark hair framed a beautiful face but tiny creases at the corners of her deep brown eyes revealed the intensity of her thoughts, "We could stash him with the animals but that doesn't resolve defending a potential attack. Besides, his insight will probably prove invaluable. He's the only one who's faced the Dark Lord, let alone defeated him."

The two *seers* sipped their tea in silence for a few minutes. Finally, Sky inquired, "Are there any defenses set up on the island?"

"The Professor and Nanchez have sensors to scan the horizon and they're monitoring the dark vectors but, no, there are no defenses. They're considering the possibilities and they were going to call Dadeus, the Keeper of the Powers on the Island of the Children."

"My teacher used to tell me that the best defense is a good offense. I think he stole that idea from sports but, in this case, I think we should heed his advice."

"I stopped through Jamaica and spoke with Simian. He said he'd be ready to help in any way he could."

"He's a wise man. We can use his strength and his vision."

"None of us has been trained in the use of any sort of weapon, except the magic rings that Dadeus gave us, which do fire a powerful blast."

"I'd hope that we'll not need weapons but we might want to have more of those available just in case."

"I'll remind Ponte."

The two women sipped a second cup of tea. Alius gazed around at the serene beauty of the temple and was warmed by the serenity of the little village. She thought about Morgan's Knot and the way of life it represented. Since the two sides joined together, the island bustled with activity to merge distinct and unique societies together and, at the same time, assumed an ambiance of unity and calm. Their missions to face danger in other places made home seem a safe haven but Adrian's insight had shaken her sense of security.

Sky seemed to be in deep meditation but her eyes opened wide and her lips curled into a small smile, "Our last confrontation used every animal we could find. I think this situation requires the predators, those animals who, alone or en masse, are bred to attack."

Alius smiled, "I see your point. With the help of the animals, we could set up a protective barrier...a gauntlet!"

"I think it's time to see our friend, Unis, again," whispered the tiny Thai woman.

The two *seers* joined hands and disappeared.

Ptolemy and the other Ministers sat at a large round table. There was mounting anger and frustration that accentuated the animosity within the group, since the invasion of the animals and the *seers* of the Light.

Zepallo was the first to speak, "We could send a mighty pulse through the vectors to destroy the Crystals on Morgan's Knot and the Island of the Children."

Ptolemy raged, "There is no guarantee that your plan would dispose of the young *seer*. They might have moved him to another location. Our plans depend on a series of coordinated engagements and we can not allow anyone to stand in our way!"

Wonac agreed, "If we are to move forward, then this young *seer* must be eliminated once and for all. He is the center of the only force on Earth that has the power and knowledge to stand in our path. Look around this facility! The destruction that his friends inflicted will take months to repair and we'll be forced to move combat coordination to yet another complex. No, our success depends on a decisive campaign."

Zepallo smiled, "Then let the Council move to organize our forces for an invasion of Morgan's Knot. When we have control of the island, the Third Legion can take the Island of the Children. At the very least, we'll disrupt the ability of the Forces of the Light to unite against us."

Ptolemy grunted, "Let it be so!"

~

Adrian awoke to gray skies and a cold north wind rustling the branches of the tree, outside his window, with an incessant scratching, as they scuffed back and forth against the stone wall.

His confinement dragged on for days and he felt that he was finally beginning to regain some strength. Dr. Stevens visited twice a day to administer healing waters and herbal remedies, which seemed to be helping, but apprehension and anxiety settled in to bolster his gnawing guilt, which made him even more anxious for a rapid recovery, if only to help in the defense of the island. His frailty and internment in bed compelled him to focus on the worst possibilities and his senses were primed for any hint of the approach of the Dark Forces on the horizon.

One part of his mind believed that Zepallo would mount an attack at any moment and another clung to the hope that he was just being paranoid. He tried to view the situation from the Council's point of view and the only conclusion, that made any sense, was removing him as an obstacle in their campaign for world domination.

It seemed strange that the powerful and experienced *seers* of Legio Obscurum would fear a young boy, who had barely started his education in the Powers. The things that he had accomplished did not seem particularly extraordinary but everyone around him was quick to argue otherwise. He tried not to think of his time as a vapor in their lair but, during his captivity, his spirit struggled with fear and vulnerability. His insecruity had been mounting, since he left the little house on the bay, and his current detention seemed an extension of that affliction.

For the first time, since his arrival on the island, his survival was in the hands of all those who were caring for him, a kindness that he did not wish to prolong. He had great faith in the talents of his fellow *seers* and the Keepers of the Powers but he wanted to participate, to contribute his own abilities to defend his new home, his family, his friends, and everything he believed to be right and true.

Adrian grasped that he, and he alone, brought this threat to Morgan's Knot and it was his duty to stand against Zepallo and his comrades. If there was to be a battle between the Darkness and the Light, he would be at the center. Somehow, he had become an icon of frustration for the Dark Forces and a symbol of hope to those who defended the Light. Despite his frailty, he could not hide from this challenge. The future of everything that he believed in depended on his participation.

~

Dadeus' image appeared before the *messenger*, "I'm sorry to have taken so long to get back to you but I've done some research and I think that we can supply a larger version of those rings that I supplied to our *seers*."

Ponte grinned, "All of this is based on a suspicion, a hunch if you will, that they will mount an attack at some point in the near future. If Adrian is correct, then we should expect the first assault to be on

Morgan's Knot but all of us should prepare for the possibility that they will include the Island of the Children in their plans."

"There can be no doubt about that. We've got everyone on high alert. We'll prepare for the worst and hope for the best. How's Adrian's recovery coming along?"

"Sara seems to think that he's beginning to regain a bit of strength but Dr. Stevens has insisted that he stay in bed, for the time being."

"Have you considered moving him to someplace safer," inquired the bald Keeper.

"We have but it brings up several challenges. First, where on the face of the Earth could we stash him, where he would truly be safe? Add the thought that the Dark Forces will not hesitate to destroy the island, whether he's here or not. Finally, if anyone can see through the veil of Darkness, it's Adrian. We need his talents and his insight."

Dadeus bowed his head, for a moment, considering Ponte's comments before responding, "I have to agree and I can't argue with any of it. As Adrian too often says, 'There is no other choice.' I'll send along the plans that I've developed for the crystal canons. Let me know what you think and whether there might be any improvements that I've overlooked."

"We'll get back to you as soon as we have a chance to inspect the drawings. Meantime, keep an eye out for disruptions on the vectors…light and dark!"

"Will do," smiled the blue-robed Keeper.

~

Sky and Alius landed in the meadow of the unicorns, where a long shimmering shaft of sunshine silhouetted Master Chi, stroking Unis' dazzling mane, in quiet conversation. Neither looked surprised when the *seers* materialized.

Master Chi laughed, "We've been expecting you!"

The two young women glanced at each other in astonishment, "How could you know that we were coming?"

Unis and Master Chi leaned together and laughed, "Great minds think alike!"

"You've come to discuss the possibility of revenge by the Dark Forces," said the old man. "We both came to that conclusion before we left Morgan's Knot. I'm surprised that you didn't see this possibility sooner!"

"Actually, it was Adrian who brought up the idea," replied Alius.

"That does not seem unusual, does it? Even in his delirium, he sees the potential for danger. How's he doing?"

"He's beginning to regain some strength but he's still kind of delirious and confined to bed."

"And that is as it ought to be," said Unis. "Without you, he would be a tool of destruction for Zepallo or dead."

"I feel dumb for not sensing the danger!" moaned Alius.

"You, both of you, are anything but dumb. It's just that Adrian has a unique ability to see. It's the subtle difference between looking at something and actually seeing it, just as a sculptor sees a beautiful form in a chunk of rock that most of us would pass without notice."

"Well then, if you already know why we're here, do either of you have any suggestions on how we might repulse this impending confrontation?" asked Sky.

"We do but I would like to hear your thoughts first."

"We thought about putting together an army of predators!" replied Alius.

"Then we are thinking along the same lines but there's someone that I would like to introduce you to, before we assemble our troops," smiled the old Master. "Unis has agreed to gather her friends and they'll be ready at the vent on Morgan's Knot when the time comes. In the meantime, if you will indulge me, I think that we'll all benefit from the thoughts of this person that I would like you to meet."

Unis chortled, as the Master took the hands of the two young women, "I'm afraid that we fibbed to you about this being exclusively the plane of the animals. There is one human who lives here."

Alius and Sky looked at each other, bewildered, "You mean a person lives here with the animals?"

"Yes, but only one," replied the beautiful unicorn. "Go with Master Chi and we'll meet you on the island."

The three *seers* joined hands and levitated above the forest to a bluff on the side of a huge mountain. The ocean flowed away into the horizon and seabirds of every variety swarmed around the cliff, their caws echoing off the rocks, reverberating into a beautiful chorus like the voices of a choir in a gigantic cathedral.

Without a word, the old Master turned up a rocky path through a dense forest of conifers and pines and, after a half hour, they emerged on a rocky ledge at the mouth of a large cave. The air was ripe with the intoxicating scent of burning pinion pine.

Master Chi stopped and turned to the two young women, "Please indulge me. You are about to meet the last *seer* to lead our warriors against the Dark Forces and it is most unusual for her to receive visitors."

Sky looked puzzled, "But you said that it's been a thousand years since one of the 'special ones' stood against the Dark Forces. How can this be?"

The old Master chuckled, "Each of you has learned many things about the secrets of the Powers but you've just started on your journeys to learn everything there is to know. There are many secrets yet to reveal themselves to each of us every day."

Alius was flustered, "I don't understand!"

Chi placed his hand on her shoulder, "My dear, our concept of life is only defined by the evidence we see before us, people being born and dying everywhere every day. Would you have believed that you could ride the vectors or pass between the planes, if someone had told you these things? Of course not! You would think them crazy, because there is no tangible evidence that these things are even possible. For almost everyone, they are the stuff of fantasy."

"Our concept of life is defined by the idea of being born, living for part of a century, and then greeting death. We believe because there is no evidence to the contrary. This is only one of the truths that humans have invented, contrary to natural law, when there are many other possibilities."

He locked arms with the two *seers* and guided them into the darkness. They wound their way through the twisting narrows of the cave, ducking beneath clouds of cobwebs, until they came to a cavern with a small fire burning in a pit beneath a black ceiling glistening with all of the stars in the heavens. Gentle waterfalls cascaded down the walls and songbirds provided a soft melody. A single shaft of light traced through the smoky chamber, illuminating a medallion that had been carved into the stone, a slender crescent surrounding an even-sided cross with a tiny star trying to escape near the breach.

As their eyes adjusted to the darkness, an ancient woman materialized, hovering behind the fire. A cascade of long white hair fell around her and spread out on the floor like a silk shawl, glowing in the radiance of a streak of golden brilliance. She looked up at her visitors with a warm smile, "Ah, Master Chi, I've been expecting you!"

The Master bowed to the ancient woman, "I apologize for not warning you."

"You know better than that! And who are these beautiful young women?"

"Allow me to introduce Sky and Alius. This is Orana."

The two young *seers* bowed, embraced by the old woman's silken aura flowing around them like a warm pink cloud to insulate them against the cold in the cave.

"I am pleased to meet you. From your vibrant auras, I sense that you are both very powerful *seers*."

Master Chi laughed, "They are more than capable but they still have much to learn. As you always instructed, no matter how much we learn about the Powers, there is always more!"

"And so it has always been," laughed Orana. "We all know there is a disruption in the Balance and I must assume that you are here seeking my humble advice."

"We are too obvious."

"I also sense that you have found the next 'special one'." Her green eyes twinkled, "It's about time! I have to admit that I'm getting tired and it's time for someone else to take my place!"

"You will live forever!" said Master Chi.

"That may be so but it doesn't mean that I have the energy or the will to continue with this responsibility. Do you have any idea of how old I am? I don't!" cackled the old woman, as she poked the fire with a stick, igniting a huge cloud of gold and silver sparks that billowed up to the ceiling of the cavern and exploded like tiny fireworks in a rainbow of glitter.

The Master bowed, "We hope that we've found the 'one'. He's young but he's shown great promise in standing against the Dark Lord and his forces. Unfortunately, he made the mistake of reading from Zepallo's Black Book, without supervision or protection, and it took a great army to retrieve his spirit. For the moment, he's confined to bed, until he regains his strength."

Orana snickered, "Wisdom does not come without compensation, even to the elders!"

Master Chi nodded, "This young man and his friends destroyed three of Legio Obscurum's installations but, even in his diminished state, the boy predicted the strategic necessity for revenge by Zepallo and his cronies. Thus, we're here seeking your advice on how best to defend against their impending attack."

She gazed into the fire, "You have not told me enough about this young man."

Alius spoke reverently, "His name is Adrian. He's only known about his gifts for a short time but he's accomplished some fairly astonishing things. All of his missions have involved the help of the animals."

"That's interesting and fitting. I assume that you've considered hiding this young Master and concluded that his powers will be necessary in facing this imminent battle? And it is coming, incidentally."

"I agree," replied Sky, a bit louder than she intended.

"You can speak in normal tones, my dear. I am old and rather feeble but my hearing is still functioning quite normally. Someday you'll understand some of the things that I've learned in these many years and I would hope that you treat these secrets with respect. Share them with younger *seers*, when they are ready and not before."

Sky blushed.

"Have you considered disguising him?"

The three *seers* looked at each other, without responding. In an instant, the old woman transformed herself into a panther, then a unicorn, and, finally, a tiny green tree frog flicking a ruby red tongue, before returning to her normal form, with a rousing, "Ribbit!"

"That's amazing," whispered Alius.

"Each of you has learned the lessons that have been presented to you, by your tutors or life's experience, but realize that these powers go far beyond the limitations of your education. They are only confined by your imaginations. See beyond the obvious, see what is possible, especially when it seems impossible."

Alius laughed quietly, "I don't mean to laugh at what you're saying. It just sounds very familiar. That's something that Adrian would say."

"Then you've found the one!" laughed Orana. "Let me tell you a story."

"If you look back through history, and I have seen more than my share, you'll find that every war, every battle, and every conflict was fought for at least one of only two reasons. The first is control of the

Powers and I think we all understand the consequences of that struggle," said the ancient woman emphatically.

"The second is economics. Whether the excuse was religion, or territory, or our side verses their side, good guys – bad guys, it all comes back to the accumulation and control of land and wealth. Mighty powers built their empires through the conquest of their neighbors. There is, and always has been, the need for finding and securing new sources of income, whether money, or natural resources, or water, or tillable land to provide food for their populations. Conquerors plunder their enemies, carry off their treasures, enslave their people, and absorb their cultures. Unfortunately, this is a never-ending cycle that creates the need for more land, more wealth, more of whatever they could take to shore up their powers and feed an ever-expanding populace."

"One could use the Roman Empire as an example. A tiny, but ambitious, city-state began gobbling up its neighbors but, in the process, their expansion demanded more land and farmers to produce food for the a larger population, a larger army to defend the extended borders, systems to provide clean water and carry waste away, new roads to allow the troops to move rapidly over longer distances, and a larger bureaucracy to meet the needs of the citizenry. The list goes on and on but the end result was that they had no other choice but perpetual expansion and, eventually, their borders extended from Britain to Africa, from what is now the Middle East to the Atlantic and it finally reached a critical point, where the whole system proved unsustainable and collapsed."

"History provides endless examples of groups who mastered the Dark Powers and, in every instance, they were driven to expand their influence, destroy those who might stand against them, and consolidate their authority. Power begets greed but greed has no value without power. The evil ones must dictate everything to everyone or their dominance is threatened."

"I grew up during a long period of human depravity in the Dark Ages, a name used to describe that episode of history, which offers only a hint of the true struggle that raged behind history's tales of chivalry and daring, poverty and oppression. Throughout hundreds of years, a very small caste of families controlled the governing bodies, the wealth, religion, and, what I will call, intellectual property or ideas. There were two classes in society and the poor existed only to provide for those in power."

"Those who believed in the Power of the Light were persecuted and executed with great cruelty and fanfare. The ability to read was restricted to a very small privileged portion of the population and religion was used, not only, to control the masses but as an excuse for wars that extended the dominance of the Dark Forces throughout the real world. The plunder from those wars increased the wealth and power of the few. Venice, one of my favorite cities, is decorated with treasures pillaged from Constantinople by the invaders, who launched great crusades under the guise of defending the Church."

"Two things occurred in the buildup to a final battle that culminated in the Renaissance, the rebirth of ideas and the opening of all levels of society. The first resulted from the invention of the printing press, which allowed ideas to be shared among all classes of society. Suddenly, the common man could read from the ancient texts. They could explore concepts and ideas, filtered or buried for hundreds of years, and develop and discuss new discoveries or theories. They could read from the religious tomes and began to question the authority of the clergy and those who governed them. Those who had been hiding and sharing the knowledge of the Positive Crystals began to teach, to share, and guide the people to a new understanding of the world around them."

"The entrenched powers had no choice but to fight for their survival and a confrontation was inevitable. The resulting battle is not recorded in any history book. There were wars in many places across the Earth but the real combat occurred in the planes and raged, on and off, for over one hundred years."

"I was a young girl, hardly older than either of you, when my family and our leader were slaughtered, our troops scattered and driven into hiding. I escaped to the plane of the animals, where I recruited their help for a final desperate assault on the Dark Forces.

Together, we divided and conquered their armies, destroyed their facilities, and drove them underground. As a result, the old powers crumbled and a new age dawned for all mankind."

"Over the centuries, the Evil Ones have surfaced to attempt to regain their influence over the real world and, in each case, they've been driven back to their lairs. Rather than suffering massive confrontations, they've established surrogates in governments, armies, and religious organizations to do their bidding. Legio Obscurum remains hidden behind myths and legends, invisible puppet-masters manipulating those they placed in powerful positions. Each time they've been exposed or defeated, they slipped away to begin again in a different place. Their resilience and determination is to be respected and never underestimated."

She paused, raising a crooked finger to her lips, "This confrontation will be different. They can't send the army of some proxy nation to invade your island. They're being forced to commit their own troops to fight this battle and you must use that to your advantage. They're exposing the very fabric of their authority and you have the opportunity to shred their power. It will take them a little while to organize their troops and to develop a plan. Use this time wisely. Certainly, you face a daunting threat but you must see this as an opportunity to push the Dark Forces back into their burrows for years to come."

"This war is centered around your friend and he must lead the campaign or you will fail. Hide him, disguise him, use his knowledge, his talents, and his hunches to direct your forces and then allow him to move to the front, only when he is most needed. Trust in his abilities and his instincts. From what you've told me, he's the only one who can lead you to victory." The old woman pondered the flames leaping from un-charred logs, for a moment, before breaking into the giggles of a young girl, "I wish I was a hundred years younger, I'd love to throttle those devils again!"

"If there is time and he has the strength, bring him to me. There is much that he and I need to discuss." She said, looking up at the three *seers* with the innocence of a small child radiating the fearless intensity of a Master *Seer*.

"This can be the end of times or the beginning of another thousand years, when the Light might finally shine on all mankind. Use your talents, your intelligence, and the fact that your enemies are driven by revenge. They see this as a mere step in their plans, instead of the ultimate battle for control over the Powers. Given their arrogance, they probably have no idea that you will mount a defense. They're at a disadvantage before they even start."

"There is one more thing that you should know. Zepallo is the young upstart, charging ahead with dreams of becoming king of the world. There are other, even more powerful *seers* on their Council. Ptolemy, senior among titans, for one and I'm sure there are others. Be aware that there is political warfare within the Council of Ollapez and that chink is a weakness."

The three *seers* thanked Orana for sharing her wisdom and turned to leave the cave but, before they reached the entrance, her soft voice filled the chamber, "Believe in yourselves, believe in the Light. See this as the hour before sunrise and know that all living creatures are counting on you, in this moment before the dawning of a beautiful tomorrow, even if they don't know it."

Master Chi smiled and looked down at the two young women, "I hope you understand why we must protect this very special treasure."

Alius looked into his eyes, "She is everything that we might hope to become. She is our history and I hope that we'll have another chance to meet with her. I understand, now, about the special ones."

Sky hugged her friends, "I feel privileged. We have much to do."

Master Chi escorted them back to the meadow of the unicorns, where they found Unis waiting. "You'll have the help you need but there is one more thing. When we left Morgan's Knot, we realized that there is a direct link between the island and the plane of the animals. I would suggest we move Adrian into the plane, where he can guide your forces and still be out of harm's way. It would be helpful if we could disguise him as one of us."

"We'll talk with him," said Alius. "Send an emissary to the island to coordinate our efforts."

Unis smiled, "We'll be there when you need us."

Sky turned to Alius, "There are other people I need to see before we enter this battle. I'll meet you on the island when I'm finished. In the meantime, talk with Adrian and tell him what we've learned."

Alius hugged the tiny *seer* and then Master Chi, "Thank you…both of you."

The Master stared into her eyes with empathy, "This is not your battle. It's a war between the Light and the Dark and we will all be with you in this fight. Be safe on your journey home."

Chapter Eight

Alius soared from the plane of the animals through the vectors to the island, pondering her first encounter with Orana, sage of the heritage that they were trying to protect and everything a young woman *seer* might hope to attain in her life. She was captivated by the impish glee of a young girl in those ancient knowing eyes, yet her bearing revealed the serene assurance of a fierce warrior…strong, devious, conniving, focused, and open to everything around her. Perhaps these things come with living to be over a thousand years old but Alius suspected that the ancient *seer* probably displayed these same qualities as a precocious child fighting carnage and oppression.

Low clouds parted and an orange sun peeked over the horizon to fire the garden at the House of the Four Seasons, which was full and lush in spite of the frigid temperatures, in a warm pool of light. She turned to find Adrian sitting with the twins on the split log benches near the kitchen door.

The patient stood painfully, as she walked over for a hug, "I'm surprised to see you up and about."

"Well, I'm up but I've been told that I can't be about yet! There's so much to do!"

"Sit down, I have some things we need to talk about."

She hugged Molly and Megan and asked, "Has he been behaving himself?"

Molly giggled, "After being confined for days, he's turned into a cranky male person, who's been demanding to be allowed outside, even if it is freezing out here."

Megan added, "We thought about sitting on him but it wouldn't have done any good. He'd just levitate us or vanish into the vectors."

"Or worse," Alius smirked briefly, before her eyes focused on Adrian, noticing a bit of pink in his pale cheeks. "I've just come from meeting with Master Chi and Sky. The Master took us to meet the oldest woman in the world…well, not our world…in the plane of the animals."

"You mean a human actually lives there?" inquired Adrian.

"Yes, but only one and, after meeting her, I understand why," smiled Alius. "She was the 'special one' who stood against the Dark Forces and defeated them, a thousand years ago, and led all the battles since."

"How can that be?" asked an astonished Megan.

"I honestly don't have a clue but I really believe the things she told us and have no doubt that she is ancient."

"Wow," whispered Molly. "So, what's her name?"

"Orana."

Adrian stared inquisitively, "Why didn't we know about her and what did she say?"

Alius recounted their conversation and ended by saying, "I know you don't like the notoriety of being a hero and a celebrity but we're all pretty sure that you are the 'special one' of our time and I believe that you can lead us to victory in this battle that is sure to come. Orana suggested we disguise you, until we need you at the front, so my question is…if you could be any animal, what would you be?"

Adrian mulled the question for a moment, staring up at streaks of light fanning across the sky. "An eagle," he replied, grinning. "I've always been envious of Magnus' ability to hang in the air."

"I knew you'd say that," laughed Alius. "Then you'll become an eagle!"

Adrian blushed, then grinned at the thought of being able to fly like his friend Magnus. "I think I could use some lessons from a real eagle."

"Orana wants to meet you. She said that you two have much to discuss."

"I'm not sure I'm strong enough to make that journey yet, but I'm getting better. I guess everything depends on how much time we have, before the Dark Forces appear on the horizon."

"Oh, I almost forgot," said Megan, "Dadeus is at the Professor's, along with Simian and Sammy. They asked us to send you to them, as soon as you got back."

"I'll go check in but I'll be back in a little while," smiled the blond *seer*, as she touched Adrian's cheek with a crooked finger, bowed her head, and disappeared.

~

Ester opened the door to the observatory and enveloped Alius in a hug, "I've been worried about you!"

The little *seer* whispered, "When there is time, I have to tell you about the woman I met. She reminded me of you!"

Ester stretched her thin lips across her too small teeth in a loving smile, "Come in, come in. It's cold out there and we have some people in the parlor, who want to meet you."

Alius stepped across the threshold, amazed to find the library crammed with a diverse collection of people. The faces of Dadeus, Gabrielle, Mary, Raffe, Simian, and Sammy appeared through the crowd. An old Chinese man was talking quietly with one of the tiny old people with the funny hats, from South America, who helped rescue Adrian. Shambala was introducing a very tall black man to a pair of American Indians in flowing headdresses of eagle feathers. Yellow-robed monks mingled with an Eskimo, two Japanese women, and a man, who wore a very formal suit and carried a black bowler hat. The little *seer* guessed he might be English but hearing an accent in the din of the chatter in a dozen languages was impossible.

Sammy wandered from one discussion to the next with the delight of a child in the world's most intriguing toy store, adding comments and asking questions as he went. His elders listened with respect and Alius was sure he was well on his way to becoming a knowledgeable Keeper.

Everywhere she looked, there were strange combinations of people of different backgrounds and ethnicities and she realized these were Keepers of the Powers from every corner of the world. An intense energy permeated the crowd, adding to her confidence that they would have help and expertise to defend against the Dark Forces.

Ponte, wearing a deep burgundy waistcoat with an electric blue bow tie, emerged from the elevator with a monk and a slender man in a turban and spied Alius across the room. He waddled through the crowd to wrap her in a big hug, "We've found some help with the technical end of things but I'm glad to see you're back safe and sound. How was your journey?"

"I don't think this is the moment to go into detail but I learned more than I ever might have hoped and we'll have the troops we need to defend the island against the attack, when it comes."

The Professor smiled, "I do want to hear your tale, when there is a moment."

Alius kissed his cheek, as he turned away, raising his hands in the air and bellowing, "Your attention, please!"

The noise of conversation died down and everyone focused on Ponte. "I must say that I'm delighted and thankful that all of you are here to help in this endeavor. After talking with many of you, it strikes me that we've all found different ways of using the Powers in positive and constructive ways. Now we're confronted with defending all that we've built over generations and our focus must adjust to include defensive and offensive weapons. I will suggest that we break up into groups of four or five to explore various options but first, I would like to introduce one of our young *seers*, Alius, who is just back from a journey to seek help in this battle."

Without warning, he turned to Alius and wrapped an arm around her shoulders, "Tell us what you've found."

Alius blushed, not accustomed to speaking to large groups of people, "I'm just back from visiting the plane of the animals and I've been assured that we will have their help, when the time comes. I also met a very old *seer* named Orana…"

A murmur rippled through her audience and Alius was instantly aware that the old *seer's* eminence was more than legend to this group. "She told me that we can and must defeat the Dark Forces and she confirmed that we have in our midst the 'special one', who will stand in her place during this battle. He is recovering from having his essence kidnapped by Zepallo but he'll be ready and more than willing to lead us."

A voice shouted, "How can we be sure that he is the one?"

"You can only believe what Orana confirmed. I trust that her reputation and her place in our legacy is enough for the moment."

"When will we meet this *seer* that you spoke of?" inquired the Englishman.

"I've just come from him and he's beginning to regain some strength. He'll be ready when we need him. In the meantime, the animals from the plane have suggested that we disguise him as an animal until the decisive moment."

"He should be at the front! Leaders lead!" commented an Indian gentleman.

"He's responsible for destroying two of their facilities, connecting all of the nodes, and embarrassing the Dark Lord in front of the whole world. That's reason enough for their impending attack. Their objective is to eliminate him and we can not allow that to happen," responded Alius in a strong and clear voice. No one could doubt that, despite her diminutive size or her tender age, she was in charge of this gathering and would not be swayed by her elders.

She continued, "Professor Ponte, Nanchez, Sammy, and Dadeus are familiar with this island and the Powers of our Crystals. I would suggest that the rest of the Keepers coordinate with them. While you're doing that, I would like to meet with the *seers*."

Quiet comments buzzed through the crowd but no one voiced any objections. Mary, Raffe, Simian, Shambala, Lala, and Maze moved through the throng to join Alius.

"It's kind of crowded in here. Why don't we go up to the observatory?" suggested Mary.

"Good idea," smiled Alius.

They pushed through the chattering mob to the elevator and ascended to the quiet of the dome, settling in chairs and on pillows scattered on the floor beneath the giant telescope. The chamber was cold and dark, illuminated by light seeping through seams in the dome and orange *orbs* in the floor, around the circumference of the room. Alius distributed a pile of blankets to her friends.

"Tell us about Orana," insisted Shambala. "That's a name that I've heard whispered since I was a little girl. I always thought she was an ancient myth, you know that powerful yet feminine legend that mothers teach their daughters to emulate, but now you tell us she's alive. How can this be?"

Mary, Raffe, and Simian looked bewildered. Although they studied the Texts, they had no frame of reference for the history of the ancient *seer*. Like Adrian and Alius, their educations had, for the most part, been confined to the immediate needs of their worlds.

Alius hesitated for a moment, as she took in the expressions on the faces of her friends, "I'm not an authority on the history of the Powers but, from what I understand, Orana was a young girl...perhaps my age, during the Dark Ages, when the peasants revolted against centuries of oppression. The Forces of the Light were defeated in a giant battle and her family was murdered but she rallied the troops and the animals to win a rebellion. The Dark Forces were pushed into the shadows and are, only now, strong enough to vie for control of all of the Powers without depending on surrogates in the real world."

"I found it hard to believe that she's over a thousand years old and, yet, I honestly don't doubt it. I looked into her eyes and saw two things, a little girl and a fierce warrior. Her aura stretched out and enveloped Sky, Master Chi, and me in the warmth and passion of life."

"We talked about Adrian and whether he was the 'special one' who comes along once in a millennia. She seemed relieved that he might be the person who could finally take her place. Our planning should proceed with the assumption that he is the 'one' and our future, the future of the world for that matter, depends on protecting him. Unfortunately, I know that he'd rather lead the charge than remain in hiding. Until, he's ready, we need to be intelligent in how we manage him and our forces. I'm sure the Keepers will develop a strategy but it will be up the *seers* to fight this battle and we know that we'll be outnumbered."

"That's for sure," said Raffe, "and they've got weapons we haven't even dreamed of."

Alius continued, "Orana suggested that the Dark Forces are at a disadvantage for several reasons. First, because they don't know that we'll be waiting for them and, perhaps even more important, they're so focused on their long term goal that they'll probably treat this as a skirmish, a trivial inconvenience to clear the path for their plans."

"She suggested disguising Adrian and placing him in the plane of the animals until we need him. And, while I'm thinking about it, Unis said they found a direct link between the island and their plane, so they can be readily accessible and still remain out of sight."

Lala snickered, "Why don't we disguise ourselves, that should cause some confusion!"

Simian laughed, "Now I know why I like you so much, you're just as devious as I am!"

Maze and Lala broke into belly laughs that infected the rest of the group. Finally, Mary suggested, "I'm not sure how this works but perhaps we ought to disguise ourselves as animals common to the island…a cow, a goat, things like that. We could be in plain sight and still be invisible!"

Everyone hooted with laughter. Alius struggled to maintain her composure, to no avail. "That's brilliant. They won't know we're here until they're right upon us, the perfect ambush!"

"I have a question," said Raffe. "What about the rest of the population of the island? How are we going to protect them?"

"That's something to be considered," pondered Alius. "I honestly don't know the answer but we should get that organized as soon as possible. We don't want any civilian casualties. On the other hand, I'm sure that many of them will want to participate...to help in any way they can, so, we'll have to find a way for them to contribute. We'll know more when Sky and Master Chi get here and I'm sure the Keepers will provide some guidance."

Raffe added, "I'll be interested to hear Adrian's take on all of this. After all, you said that Orana instructed us to follow his hunches."

"I'll go back to talk with him, as soon as things are settled here. You can come along, if you like."

"You're on!" smiled Raffe. "He saved my life more than once. I owe him!"

The group descended to the parlor, where they found huddles of Keepers in deep discussions. Hands waved and voices grew loud and emphatic, as concepts and ideas were investigated, torn apart, and rebuilt.

Alius turned to Mary, "This looks as if it could go on for a while. Why don't we go visit Adrian? At least we'll have more thoughts and ideas to offer this bunch."

"Let's go," smiled Mary, ushering the other *seers* out the front door into a frosty breeze.

Nanchez pulled up in front of the observatory in his truck, which was stuffed to overflowing with a mountain of equipment. "Had enough of this bunch, have you?"

"We're just going to see Adrian. The Keepers are still in discussion and we felt we could save time and, besides, we need his input."

"Right you are! These folks will discuss until someone tells them to stop, which will probably be me, so don't be long."

"We'll see you in a little while," smiled Alius.

The *seers* joined hands and were about to move across the vectors, when Sky and Master Chi arrived. They joined the circle and flew to the House of the Four Seasons.

~

The *seers* gathered in the living room around a roaring fire in the hearth and Elsie and Sara brought snacks and drinks from the kitchen.

Adrian slumped in an overstuffed chair near the fireplace, obviously not feeling as strong as he professed.

"I guess we should report what we know, then you can tell us what you're thinking," began Alius.

"Go ahead," replied Adrian.

"Well, first, I guess I should make some introductions. You haven't met Master Chi, Shambala, Lala, and Maze, who helped rescue you. I should also introduce John and Sara, Elsie and George, and Molly and Megan to all of you."

Just then, Morgan, Kelly, Ian, Josh, and Brandy arrived and the introductions were repeated.

"The observatory is full of Keepers from every corner of the world. They're discussing the defense of the island and didn't seem ready to talk with us, so we came to see you. Orana said several things that seem important. First, that we should hide you as an animal in the plane of the animals and we've decided to disguise ourselves as domestic critters common to the island, which will allow us to hide in plain sight. The other thing she said was that you would have a unique insight into the Dark Forces. Have you any thoughts?"

Adrian grimaced, "I like your plan. While I was a puff of smoke, I saw an image of the world as it might be after the next Great War. In Zepallo's projection, the Dark Forces triumphed and the planet was a smoldering skeleton of the world we know. I watched the attacks that destroyed the Island of the Children and Morgan's Knot. The first wave of Dark Forces arrived on giant ravens, ignited a wildfire that consumed the island, and blew up the Crystals. The only survivors were those who made it to the beach to escape the inferno."

Everyone stared at Adrian. No one spoke.

"I'll be interested in what defenses the Keepers propose and I'd suggest that we get them in place as soon as possible. We can assume that it will take a little while for Legio Obscurum to mobilize their troops but I fear that we're running out of time. If they're really coming, it will be soon."

Raffe interrupted, "We had a question about the...civilians. We don't want to put them in harm's way but they built this society, so they'll probably want to defend it."

Kelly was the first to speak, "We've helped you before and we can do it again!"

Everyone laughed and patted her on the back. George stood, "We don't possess your unique talents but we all know every inch of the island, every vector point, and I'm fairly sure that everyone will want to help in any way we can."

Adrian struggled to sit upright, as he looked around at his friends and family. "I want to thank every one of you for being here, for all that you've already done, and for all that you will do in the next few days. We've had a few clashes with Zepallo and his friends and we were fortunate to win and to escape. This battle will be different. This one is about protecting our home and, ultimately, who will control the Powers. We can't allow them to defeat us, the future for everyone depends on it."

George inquired, "Has anyone given any thought to the defense of the Island of the Children? If the Dark Forces are victorious here, they'll head there next!"

The *seers* all glanced at each other before Alius replied, "I believe Dadeus and Ponte have talked about that and concluded that the first strike will be on Morgan's Knot. They want to eliminate Adrian." She looked over to Mary and Raffe, "We'll talk with Dadeus, when we get back to the observatory, to confirm that."

"I agree," said Adrian quietly, trying to conceal the fact that his energy was ebbing and failing in the charade. "They want me. I'm humbled by all of you but they have to believe that I stand in their way. I'm the target and we should use that to our advantage."

Master Chi rose, staring at Adrian, with kindness and concern, before gazing around at the group, "I agree with Adrian. Whether or not he is the 'one', they'll focus on taking him dead or alive and extraneous casualties are a bonus." He paused as everyone digested his thoughts. "We'll have at least one hundred *seers* to fight this battle but they'll have more. The animals from the plane and the animals on this island will help but the odds are in their favor. Most of you *seers* have learned about moving through the vectors and now the planes. Many of you are beginning to become proficient in levitation and I can teach you how to transform into other forms, like animals. That is not as difficult as it might sound."

Kelly piped up, "I wish I could be a fish!"

"You are a fish, when you wear your wetsuit," said Morgan.

Everyone laughed.

Master Chi stared at her beautiful smile and the watch hanging from a golden chain around her neck, "I see that you have a very special watch."

"Dr. Stevens gave it to me after we rescued Ester."

"I'd suggest that you talk with the Doctor about that watch. It has some magical properties that might prove useful in this battle."

Kelly looked mystified, as she grasped the watch to inspect the delicate hands and the intricate movement of gears and springs peeking through the carved casing, "I don't understand."

"My dear, that is a turnabout. It can be used to manipulate time."

Kelly stared at the Master and then at the beautiful watch, "He said that it was very special to him, when he gave it to me."

"You should talk with the Doctor. I'm sure there's a story behind it."

"I will."

"Now, for the moment and, until we have a chance to talk with the Keepers, I'd suggest that the 'civilians' organize to secure everything and everyone on the island. We want it to look normal but there is no reason to put anyone in harm's way. I'm sure the Keepers will need help with producing whatever they come up with for defensive and offensive weapons, so those of you who know anything about wood or metalworking, anyone who has a background in engineering of any sort, or anyone who has a military background should let us know, so we can employ your talents."

Elsie raised her hand, "With so many people contributing, we'll organize the preparation of food for the troops. We've already started and I'll talk with my friends, who will want to contribute to the cause. You can't fight a battle on an empty stomach!"

Everyone cheered. Simian piped up, "If it's half as good as the food you served at the festival, I'll volunteer twice!"

Sara laughed, "It will be that and more!"

"Alright!"

Master Chi raised his hand for quiet, "Alright, you ladies begin organizing your friends, I noticed a reaction from John and George, so you might get your comrades together with the Keepers. The rest of the *seers* will be arriving at the observatory shortly, so I'd ask the rest of you to meet me there in a little while. Brandy, you, Tic, and the children can be in charge of the animals on the island. I'd like to talk with Adrian in private, if that's alright with you?"

"I'd be happy to talk with you but I might suggest that we include Alius, because she's been organizing this whole effort."

"That would be fine," smiled the Master.

Sky hugged Adrian, "This is a conversation for the three of you. I'll take the rest of the crew back to the nuthouse at the observatory."

Suddenly, everyone was moving. Brandy walked up to rub against Alius and said, "Tell Tic what we're doing. I'll need his help."

Alius leaned down to hug the red dog, "I'll tell him as soon as I get back."

Brandy licked her and trotted out through the front door.

Morgan leaned over to kiss Alius on the cheek, "Take care of him."

The little *seer* took her hand with a gentle smile, "You and Orana share the same beautiful green eyes."

The tall girl blushed, "I so want to meet her."

"She's a tiny little woman but she's bigger than life and twice as wise."

After everyone left the room, Alius took a seat next to Adrian and Master Chi pulled up a chair to sit directly in front of them. "I think the first question is…how are you feeling?"

"I'm still weak but my brain is starting to feel normal," replied Adrian.

"I might suggest that you get some rest, after we leave. This battle is imminent and we'll need you."

Adrian smiled weakly, "I'll be ready, whenever it begins."

"Tell me a little bit more about the vision you described."

Adrian closed his eyes, thinking back to the scenes he witnessed during his terrifying excursion through Zepallo's revelations. His brow furrowed into a frown, "It started with a view from far out in space. The world was covered in a shroud of dense smoke and there were giant fires burning in all the major cities. There was a great battle between the Forces of the Light and the Dark. We were outnumbered and ultimately defeated. After a while, the clouds disappeared and I saw columns of Dark Forces moving through a deserted city. A loudspeaker blared a warning to the civilians, who were hiding underground. People joined the column and were instantly transformed into soldiers. Those with children, left them on the side of the road and marched on. The next scene was of Morgan's Knot and the animals were running across the island, ahead of a giant firestorm that burned everything. The Golden Crystal exploded and the only survivors were those who made it to the beach. A volcano erupted on the Island of the Children and the lava flowed down through the tunnels, killing everyone."

"That's interesting," mused the old *seer*. "I'm sure it was truly frightening but it was only a vision...a nightmare created by Zepallo through his Black Book. Perhaps we should view it as a prophecy...or, better, a fantasy. You must see it as one possibility of many. Although the Texts predict the future, they're not always correct. They use information that is available at the moment but everything in the future is subject to change and I have no doubt that a *seer* with Zepallo's sophistication could manipulate his book to conjure up the scenes you saw. I believe that we can alter his prediction."

Adrian looked relieved, "I feel as if I've been carrying that around like a stone on my shoulders, afraid to share it with anyone who might not understand. It's almost as if I felt I had to protect my friends and family from that possibility."

The old Master's eyes crinkled into tiny slits, "I understand how you feel but let's create our own version, shall we? We have several advantages, first, all of the people who have shown up to help...the *seers*, the Keepers, your friends and family. Second, we might suspect that the force that invades the island will be formidable but they're at a disadvantage, because they don't know that we're preparing for them and, even if they can sense your energy, they won't know exactly where to find you. Third, we have the animals from the plane, who will be withheld until they're needed."

Alius looked over at Adrian. His eyes looked tired but more confident. "What about transforming ourselves into animals? How does that work?"

Master Chi's round face lit up with an impish smile, "It's fairly simple. You've both been taught the basics of levitation...that state where you are totally focused within yourself. This is just a variation on that. Let's try an experiment. Alius, I would suggest that you imagine the most beautiful snow leopard you can imagine. She is sleek, quick, and quiet. She is sensuous, beautiful, and deadly. See this image in your mind, feel it in your heart, and know its very essence in your soul. See yourself as the snow leopard…"

Before he could finish, Alius transformed into a white leopard with golden spots, perched on the chair. She turned to Adrian and let out a ferocious roar, purred softly, then licked her lips with a long pink tongue.

"All you have to do to get back to your normal state is to let go of the vision. As soon as you release it from your mind, you'll regain your normal form."

With that, the snow leopard morphed back into a beaming Alius, "I like being a cat!"

"It suits you, my dear! Okay, now let's try Adrian. What do you want to be?"

"An eagle," smiled Adrian, who closed his eyes and concentrated on his vision of Magnus hanging in the wind. A moment later, his body contracted and transformed into a golden eagle. The giant bird let out a squawk and fluttered its wings, as it looked from Alius to the Master with piercing amber eyes. A moment later, Adrian reappeared. "That's wonderful. I thought about trying to fly but I was pretty sure that I'd destroy the room!"

Alius and Master Chi laughed. "I think you've got the idea. Is there an eagle on the island?"

"Yes, a very special eagle. His name is Magnus."

"I'd suggest that you take some lessons from him before the battle begins."

"I'll find him," smiled Adrian.

"Do you have any other insights that we ought to consider?"

Alius interrupted, "I've noticed something about their troops during our confrontations in the Caucasus and in New York. They're afraid of their leaders. That's not to take anything from their abilities but I just felt that the alternative to fighting might be worse than the battle."

"That's interesting," injected Adrian. "I felt the same thing. I also sensed that there was a conflict between some of the leaders, while

I was being held captive in that *orb* sitting at the middle of the their conference table. It was almost as if different factions were pulling against each other, although I couldn't tell who was arguing about what."

"That doesn't surprise me," replied the old Thai Master, as he rubbed his round tummy in contemplation. "There are rumors of power struggles between different blocs, persistent rival families and factions that have vied with each other for centuries. Considering the fact that Zepallo has been so public in his efforts, Orana suggested that he does not have the full support of the other dark *seers* and that there are other, perhaps, more powerful *seers* on their Council. He's a renegade who seeks ultimate personal power. That division could be to our advantage."

"If ever I wished to be a fly on the wall, this might be it," smirked Alius.

Master Chi laughed, "Well, let's pretend that you are a fly on that wall. From what Adrian has told us, we might assume that their impending invasion is a compromise between at least two sides. Eliminate this young *seer*, so their mutual objectives can be fulfilled, but one side is joining in this effort reluctantly. If we can deal them a mighty blow, they might just retreat."

Adrian slumped, "Don't underestimate their abilities or their dedication to their ultimate goal. They see me as a monumental nuisance, a barrier to the next phase in their plans. It seems to me there are two possibilities. First, that they can't find me, so they can't dispose of me, but that would lead to the destruction of the island and every other outpost on the planet…or, second, they are drawn into a trap that uses their tunnel-vision to our advantage. Perhaps it is a combination of the two."

Master Chi smiled, "I think you've seen beyond the obvious. We'll hide you in the plane of the animals until we need you. Let's draw them in before we unleash our counter-attack. I also suspect that they'll come in waves, so we should allow the first group to feel confident during the initial assault."

Adrian took a deep breath, "That puts a lot of our friends in danger. I'd hope we could hide and protect as many as possible."

"We should make it appear that everything is normal on the island for as long as we can," suggested Alius. "The longer we wait, the better the chance they'll be drawn into our trap."

"I agree," replied Master Chi. "Unless you have something else to add, I think that we should return to the observatory and you should get some rest. This invasion will happen sooner than we might hope and I want you as ready as you can be, when the time comes."

Adrian stood, unsteadily, and turned to Alius, "I'm sure they'll send scouts to check out the island before they invade. That time Zepallo appeared near the observatory, he sent ravens to keep an eye on us. We should be on the lookout. Also, there's a missing ingredient in all of this and that's humor. In every mission that we've attempted, we found a way to include that little something extra that added fun to the danger and relieved the tension we all felt. I'm afraid I'm not feeling terribly creative at the moment, so perhaps you can come up with something."

Alius smiled, "I know exactly what you mean and I'll see what we can create."

Adrian added, "See if you can pass the word to Magnus. Send him here as soon as possible."

"I can do that," replied Alius, leaning into Adrian to kiss his forehead. "We will win this, I promise!"

Master Chi reached beneath his robes and offered the handle of a sword to Adrian. He pressed a blue stone on the grip and a gleaming blade, faceted from a Golden Crystal, slid into place. Adrian reached out to take the weapon. The grip was gold and inset with glowing gems of brilliant colors. He looked at the old *seer*, "This is beautiful."

"It is the sword that Orana carried against the Dark Forces centuries ago. Be careful for, not only is it a sword, but if you press the red Crystal near the guard on the handle, it will fire a powerful blast."

Adrian admired the blade and smiled, "I can only hope that it brings the luck she enjoyed!"

"You'll find that it collapses to make it easier and less dangerous to carry," replied the Master, taking the sword to press the blue crystal on the handle again. The blade retracted into the hilt. "Use it well, for this will be your best defense, until you've mastered your ultimate powers."

The old *seer* reached to place a hand on Adrian's shoulder, "I know that you're not as strong as you might hope. By tomorrow, the island will be fortified by an army of *seers,* who will work with the Keepers and your friends to deflect the attack. At all times, you must remain calm within yourself. The outcome of this battle will depend on your ability to focus your mind and your powers. If you truly believe, then no one can defeat you!"

Alius and Master Chi left for the observatory and Adrian slowly climbed the stairs to his room and collapsed on his bed.

Chapter Nine

Zepallo sat with the other Ministers at the round table in the Masters' chamber beneath the lake in the Caucasus Mountains. Massive sump pumps labored to siphon water from the lower levels of the complex but many of the systems were beginning to sputter to life, in spite of devastating damage.

"Our troops are assembling. We should be ready to begin tomorrow evening."

Ptolemy snarled, "I want to be sure that everything is in place before this campaign gets underway. I expect each action to adhere to the protocols and directives approved by this Council and the edicts of our emissaries. We've suffered enough damage and defeats at the hands of this young *seer* and I won't have those mistakes repeated!"

"A squadron of ravens have already commenced reconnaissance runs over the island," replied Zepallo. "So far, no defensive preparations have been observed and there is no reason to believe they suspect what is to come."

"When do you plan to invade?"

"Tomorrow at dusk," smiled Zepallo. "Just as the sun is setting, a mighty storm will appear in the east, more fierce than any in generations and perfect cover for the assault."

"You've failed several times in your quest to turn this young *seer* to secure your own station. Let us not repeat our lapses. We must stand together as a unified force with a single goal…the elimination of the *seer* and decapitation of the Forces of Light. Once that is accomplished, we will withdraw and proceed with our plans and your career will advance at the will of the Council. Is that understood?"

"Agreed," smiled Zepallo.

Wonac hissed, "I've taken personal command to organize the troops. We'll send in three waves. If the first is successful, then we won't need to expose the rest of our warriors to unnecessary risk. Our primary objectives are finding the child and destroying the Golden Crystal. It does not matter whether we capture or kill the young *seer*. Either will suffice."

Ptolemy shouted, "I don't want a prisoner! I want this problem solved once and for all!"

Wonac bowed, "As you wish, Master."

"Then it's settled, we attack tomorrow night. I want to see the final reconnaissance reports before our troops begin the assault!"

~

Sara tiptoed up to Adrian's room and held her finger to her lips. The door eased open without a sound and she peaked around the edge, hoping to let him rest, if he was asleep, but gaped in astonishment at a golden eagle perched on his headboard. The beautiful bird squawked loudly and fluttered its wings, as she slipped into the room.

"Adrian, is that you?"

The giant bird glanced up with blazing golden eyes and melted into the young *seer's* normal form. "I'm sorry, I didn't mean to scare you. I was just practicing."

"That's pretty amazing," laughed his mother. "I'm not really sure which you I like best!"

Adrian pouted.

"Magnus has been sitting in the tree outside your window for about a half an hour. He told Molly that you'd asked him to come."

Adrian turned to open the window, finding the magnificent eagle sitting patiently on a branch outside. "I'm sorry, I didn't realize you were here. Come in," said Adrian.

The eagle glided through the opening and landed on the back of his desk chair, "I'm not used to flying inside a house. I might break something!"

"Relax," smiled Adrian. "I just want to ask you for some coaching on how to be an eagle!"

Sara walked over to close the window and returned to stroke the beautiful bird's feathers. "You are a wonder!"

"I've had practice," squawked Magnus. "The trick will be to train Adrian to, not only, act like an eagle but to think like one too. I understand we probably don't have much time."

"I'm afraid you're right," replied Adrian. "The plan is to hide me in the plane of the animals until the invasion begins. I'll need to be ready to move at the right moment."

"Well, let's see what you look like as an eagle."

Adrian calmed himself and concentrated. A moment later, he morphed into an eagle that looked almost exactly like Magnus. "I'm sorry I took your form but you're the only example I have in my mind," squawked Adrian.

Magnus looked him over and fluttered, "Well, it's not perfect but pretty close. I am a handsome bird, if I do say so myself!"

Sara laughed, gazing back and forth between the two eagles, who looked perfectly comfortable perched in Adrian's bedroom. "I'm sorry but this situation looks so odd!"

Adrian transformed back into his human form, "I've always been envious of your ability to soar on the wind!"

"That's an easy one," replied Magnus. "It's even more fun to tuck your wings into your body and dive on a quarry."

Adrian smiled, "I think I'll need some practice."

"Before we go, you have to understand the way of an eagle. We are the masters of the sky. No other creature can fly as high or as fast, except, perhaps, our cousins the peregrines. I think our most enviable quality is that we're highly intelligent and possess an inner strength and determination that is unmatched in nature. You have to be strong of heart, fearless, and proud!"

Sara looked at her son, "I think you possess all of those qualities. You chose the right animal as your disguise."

Adrian gave her a big hug.

"Are you sure that you're up to this?" inquired his mother.

"I have no choice. It's now or never," smirked Adrian. "It always seems to end up this way, doesn't it?"

Sara kissed him on the forehead and opened the window. Adrian transformed back into an eagle, hopped onto the sill, and raised his wings to follow Magnus into the evening sky.

In a minor panic, the boy wanted to flap his wings as fast as possible but mirrored the rhythm of Magnus' long slow strokes, as they scooped up the air, gaining altitude and speed. Magnus closed on his student, "Are you okay?"

He felt more alive and connected to his body than he had since his rescue and was not surprised to find that flying was way more fun than walking, "I'm fine. Teach me how to hang in the air."

Magnus squawked, "Turn into the wind."

Adrian tipped a wing and banked into the setting sun. The wind out of the west was fairly steady and he hooked his wings to hang in midair.

"I think you've got it. Adjust your wing tips to hold yourself in position and tilt the back of your wings down just a little."

Adrian made the adjustments and found that he could hang almost perfectly still without expending any energy. He looked out over the ridge to the setting sun oozing into the sea, the sky streaked with crimson and amber, and he felt that nothing in the world could be more serene.

"Now let's try diving. When we're ready, pull your wings in close to your body and point yourself at a target on the ground. Instead of using the full extent of your wings, just use the primary feathers at the tips and your tail to maintain your trajectory. When you're almost on your quarry, flare your wings, just as we're doing now, and adjust your flight path with your tail to scoop up our dinner. Make sure you're ready, because the deceleration is abrupt, and don't wait too long as I did, when I was young and foolish and completely lost control. Fortunately, I hit some springy trees that pitched me back up in the air but it was most embarrassing! It's certainly not something you want to do more than once, if you can help it!"

Adrian laughed, tucked his wings close to his body, and pointed himself at a rabbit scurrying through a field to the south of the foundry. The crisp clarity of his vision was amazing, as if everything was focused and magnified to the point he could see several field mice darting out of the path of the rabbit.

He dove within feet of the cottontail and extended his wings, stretched his talons, then swooped just above the scampering quarry and soared back into the air. "That was fantastic!" he yelled to Magnus.

"Well done!" replied the beautiful eagle. "You could have had him!"

"I don't think I'm a hunter at heart," smiled Adrian. "I love all of you too much to harm any of you!"

"I suspect your feelings are part of the reason that you're becoming such a powerful *seer*. It is as it should be," squawked the eagle, looping around Adrian to guide him to the south. "Let's make a run to the tip of the island and then I think you ought to head back for some rest. The bad guys are going to arrive soon enough."

The two eagles soared at top speed along the thermals rising up from the ridge through the last golden rays of dusk, circled above the jagged tail of the island, and skimmed just above the crests of waves crashing on the rocky shoreline on the west side of the island, the water splattering glistening bursts in the fading light. The windows of the little houses dotting the hillside were beginning to glow, as *orbs* were lit and preparations for the evening meal begun. Adrian looked over at Magnus, "It all seems so peaceful. Let's hope it's still this beautiful after whatever's coming."

"If we all do our parts, it will be," replied Magnus.

They flew over the school and down to the House of the Four Seasons, landing just outside the vegetable garden. Adrian morphed back into his normal form, "Thank you, but I'm more envious than ever!"

"Well, it was short but you understand the basics. We'll fly together again tomorrow."

"Keep an eye out for ravens. I suspect they'll send in spies before the attack. It would be helpful if you could interfere with their reconnaissance."

"I'll get with the hawks to ensure we have scouts flying and we'll let you know what's happening when they reveal themselves. That will be your cue to move to the plane of the animals and I'll accompany you."

"Great, I'll see you tomorrow and thanks again!"

"You're welcome," said Magnus, as he raised his wings and lifted off across the fields towards the coast.

~

Alius arrived back at the observatory to find the Keepers deep in consultation. Ponte turned to greet her, "This is amazing! So many creative minds working on the same puzzle!"

"It's time to stop talking and start our preparations. George and John are organizing the citizens. Sara and Elsie are talking with the other ladies about preparing mountains of food for the troops and Adrian asked me to add one more element to the equation…humor!"

Ponte's eyes twinkled. Although he was many years Alius' senior, she always suspected a mischievous little boy was hiding inside the chubby body of the brilliant old Keeper.

"Oh, I think we can do that!" laughed the Professor, peeking over the top of his little glasses.

"Sometimes, you scare me!" giggled Alius.

"Your attention, please," called Ponte. The raucous crowd was obediently silent, as they turned to listen. "I'm afraid that we've run out of time, we must begin our preparations. Nanchez has set up a series of *messengers* to monitor the vectors, both light and dark, for any disruptions by the Dark Forces. We also have crystals of every size and color, tools in the workshop, a foundry just down the coast, and a force of people to help with any construction that might be needed. Now what have you come up with?"

The English gentleman held his bowler to his chest, as he stood, "We suggest an energy curtain surrounding the island. It won't stop them but it should slow them down and inhibit their ability to monitor the island and communicate with each other."

Ponte looked across the room to Nanchez, "Do we have the power?"

"I'm not sure we do. We could use one Crystal to shield the observatory and, perhaps, the House of the Four Seasons. I doubt we have the energy for more than specific targets."

"Who else?"

The light cascading down from the stars in the ceiling reflected bright speckles on Dadeus' bald head. "We can produce as many blaster rings as you might need and our little group here has revised the original concept drawings for producing crystal canons that will have the same effect on a much larger scale."

"Great, get your people together with John and George. They can supply any materials you might need, plus they're both more than capable of helping with design and construction, and Samuel can forge almost anything in the foundry. Adrian has suggested that we incorporate a little humor in our efforts. Does anyone have any thoughts on that?

Shambala, Sky, and the other *seers* emerged from the elevator, "We've been talking about disguising ourselves as animals common to the island but that's not set in stone. We're open to suggestions!"

Ponte laughed, "I have a plan for you!"

Sky walked over to Alius and whispered, "The rest of the *seers* will be here at dawn tomorrow."

Alius leaned over to the tiny *seer*, "Great!" She raised her hand for quiet, "Has anyone given any thought to defending the Island of the Children?"

Dadeus stood, "I've been in touch with Gabrielle and our technicians on the island and they are aware of the situation. They're constructing defenses but, it seems to me, the initial thrust of the attack will be here on Morgan's Knot. If their goal is to eliminate Adrian, they will strike here first."

"Agreed!" murmured the crowd.

The discussion went on for thirty minutes, as ideas were considered, accepted and put into action, or discarded. Finally, Ponte interrupted an ancient Keeper from southern Africa, who was droning on and on. "Time is of the essence. Everything that we are proposing has to be finished and in place before dawn tomorrow. We want them to think that everything is normal on the island and that we have no idea that they're coming, so stealth is of the essence! Places everyone!"

~

As the sun crested the horizon, five ravens skimmed endless white caps rolling towards Morgan's Knot. The formation soared over the southern tip of the island and headed north along the eastern coast. A few farmers were heading out to their fields and the farm animals sauntered through tall grasses to their keepers, anxious for some breakfast.

As the black birds approached the observatory, they turned east to survey the little village in the crook of the cove and were surprised to find a large round red and yellow tent with circus animals milling about the meadows west of the shops. A large cannon had been erected to fire a human into a giant net suspended from tall poles and workmen were raising a Ferris wheel, along with a roller coaster, a winding go-cart track, and several other rides.

Magnus and Harriet, the hawk, led clouds of seagulls, herons, pelicans, pipers, robins, cardinals, blue jays, crows, owls, and scores of smaller birds dropping out of the sun to attack from above and below. The ravens veered east, harassed by the giant flock until they were out of sight of land.

As their tormentors turned back to Morgan's Knot, the giant black birds slipped into the plane of the dark vectors and zoomed to the lair in the Caucasus Mountains. Zepallo was alone in the Master's chambers, when two guards escorted them into the room.

"What have you found?"

The dominant raven panted and his black eyes blazed, "We were attacked by a large flock of birds from the island, so we didn't get to view everything but...we did see a large tent and circus animals. It appears that they are preparing for some sort of carnival."

Zepallo smiled, "You saw no other preparations or defenses."

"No, sir. We did not."

"Perfect. It appears they have no idea that we're coming. This might be easier than we thought. Gather your flock. We'll attack at sunset!"

The Dark Lord pushed through the doors and strode along the hallway to the dome, where technicians were preparing to create the large storm and coordinating communications with squadrons of warriors. Their broken systems had been adequately patched together to connect with the dark network for the campaign.

Ptolemy and Wonac stood on the podium, orchestrating the efforts of the technicians, as Zepallo entered. "What have you learned?"

The Evil One looked up with an engaging smile, "It seems they're preparing for a circus! They have no idea!"

"Then let us begin placing our troops in ready positions," replied Ptolemy, his old face crinkled into a sinister smile. "I look forward to our complete success!"

"And so it shall be," laughed Wonac, who never laughed.

A brilliant sun dragged across the sky in slow motion and the tension washed across the island, as everyone waited anxiously for the battle to begin. A few wondered whether Adrian's hunch might have been the ravings of a disturbed boy, who suffered who-knows-what while he was captive in that cavern, but none were quite ready to abandon their duties.

Magnus reported that the ravens had been allowed to scan the eastern shore of the island, before being diverted out to sea. He and Adrian withdrew to the vent on the ridge behind the barn at the House of the Four Seasons.

Ponte's circus proved a clever diversion, soliciting the help of the appropriate animals from the plane and disguising many of the residents of the island to fit with the theme.

Travis maintained an observant vigil with Mary, Morgan, Molly, Megan, Josh, Ian, and Raffe in the fish shop, at the direction of the Elders, monitoring sensors along the beaches, the bluffs, and the little cove, should the Dark Forces arrive by sea. They would avoid the western side of the island, which offered only a steep, craggy coastline and the ridge blocking access to the eastern plain. Each of the children had been armed with blaster rings, several of Ponte's improved flashpans, and a clever energy shield that extended from a band they wore on their wrists.

Some of the visiting Keepers wore heavy work clothing, normal to the island, and wandered near their installations, pretending to tend the animals or ready harvesters to bring in the grains growing in the fields. Sammy took charge of the installations along the ridge and coordinated his group with quiet confidence. Everyone had been evacuated from the House of the Four Seasons, with the exception of Tic and Brandy, who lounged in the shade of the front porch with a clear view across the fields to the bluffs. When the time came, they would direct the *seers* and animals hiding in the forest for the defense of the old farmhouse.

Alius, Simian, Sky, and Master Chi huddled in the parlor of the observatory, while Ponte monitored the *messengers* for disruptions in the planes. Nanchez and Dadeus moved to the mountain to prepare the circuits from the Black Crystal.

"The ravens were here this morning. I'd have suspected an attack sooner," pondered Alius.

"If they don't come today, they'll come tomorrow," sighed Simian, stroking his little goatee. "Patience my young friend."

Master Chi and Sky floated a foot above the floor in front of fuming embers barely glowing in the fireplace, meditating together in search of fluctuations in the tones of the energies. Their eyes opened, just as Ponte barked, "We've got a storm forming to the east!"

"We don't get storms from the east. They always come from the northwest," replied Ester.

"They're coming," whispered Sky, as she settled back on the carpet. "It's time!"

~

A cluster of thunderheads billowed up from a calm sea, boiling into the sky. A liquid orange sun drooped over the ridge, oozing a fiery glow under the clouds that revealed the core of the storm, a raging inferno exploding into the heavens. Slowly, the formation swelled into a swirling squall, churning the cold waters of the Atlantic into a tsunami.

Torrents of rain flashed in brilliant curtains of lightning, crackling with the radiance of a thousand suns. Thunder rumbled with the tenor of a crumbling mountain and rolled into the dying moan of a wounded demon echoing across the island. Behind the furious façade, waves of dark cloaked troops flew in tight formation on the wings of giant ravens above small silent submarines skimming just beneath the surface, swarming north and south to surround the island and deliver squads of warriors.

Zepallo appeared in the clouds to direct the troops through a communicator in his right ear. "Your instruments should display the primary target as the farmhouse on a bluff overlooking the eastern plain, three miles to the southwest of the little village. The second objective is the tower of black stone, with the silver dome of an observatory on top, located below the ridge to the south of the volcanic mountain. The

Golden Crystal is beneath it. We will divide into two columns, the first positioned to attack from the south and advance on the farmhouse, while the other joins with our troops, arriving on the submarines, and moves through the little village to converge on the observatory. Find and kill the young *seer*, destroy the Crystal, and we can all go home!"

The troops cheered and flew to the west at top speed.

~

Adrian dressed in his blue robes and spent an hour alone in his room, calming his mind and struggling to energize his body. He focused on the strength and majesty of an eagle but, in his meditation, a vision of a panther slinking silently through the darkness of the jungle, its golden eyes glowing with cunning focus and ferocious intensity, roared through his mind. He smiled to himself, *"You can't fight this battle in the darkness. At some point you'll have to show yourself and then you'll be mine!"*

He was surprised to find the plane of the animals touched the forest along the ridge running the length of the island from north to south, something that should have been obvious to a sensitive and observant *seer* long ago. He and Magnus sat in the branches of a hulking burr oak that allowed an unobstructed view of the fields along the eastern side of the isle.

He felt like a cloud in the sky overlooking his home before Captain Morgan brought those first families from the mainland. In this dimension, there were no roads or houses, no sign of human activity, for this was the island as it might have been, had his ancestors never found or developed the magic and the Balance. The details of both dimensions seemed to overlap and, although he couldn't see the people on the island, he was aware of the glow of their auras moving through the landscape. He could only hope that the dark *seers* did not sense their energies.

This particular tree grew at an entry into a breach in the planes, which would allow instant access when they were needed. A large storm, erupting on the eastern horizon, reflected the blazing sunset in an enormous inferno rising to blot out the sky.

Adrian whispered, "They're coming."

"Hang on. We don't want to move until the last moment. You'll have to be patient and think like an eagle!" instructed Magnus.

Adrian looked along columns of animals, hidden in the trees for as far as he could see in either direction. Unis was directly beneath him. "They're coming," he called.

"We all feel their approach," replied the beautiful unicorn. "It's a bitter wind that precedes them!"

"Are all of you ready?"

"We're ready when you are!"

Adrian turned back to the writhing storm charging the savage surf rolling onshore. Lightning crackled and thunder tumbled across the island, beckoning him to action. He fought to quiet those shrieking voices inside his head, to remain quiet and still. A surge coursed through is body and he wondered whether it was anticipation of the coming battle or the first hint of that charge that raced up his spine, whenever Zepallo was near. Whatever the source, he was ready and anxious to begin.

Ponte punched a code into the *messenger* and a glowing image of Nanchez and Dadeus appeared. The Professor smiled, "Let the fun begin!"

Nanchez grinned, "The system is primed and ready!"

He tapped a few keys and Travis flashed before the screen. "Let the swimmers go!"

"They're on their way," replied Travis.

Another code and little Kelly appeared, "Are you ready?"

Kelly smiled, "Dr. Stevens and I are ready when you are."

"Hold the animals until the troops approach their targets. Don't move too soon or you'll give them an advantage."

"I've done this before," smiled Kelly, holding the gold watch up to the tiny *messenger* on her wrist.

A final call to the group gathered in the village and the circus tent, "Are you ready?"

George's face appeared covered with white greasepaint and a large red bulbous nose, "If we don't start soon, this is going to turn into a fairly wild party!"

"Right! Hold tight until the appropriate moment!"

"Can do!"

~

Nanchez hesitated for an instant, remembering the last time he made these connections. So much had changed on the island in these few short months. Now the objective was different but the process remained the same. He pressed a pulsing tab on his console.

Crystals and *orbs* flickered and flashed, as the system powered up and the sequence surged energy through the filters. A warm gale whistled out of the west and massive clouds swelled over the sea. Lightning shimmered and thunder growled, as the Nanchez' storm billowed up over the ridge, a phantom ghoul silhouetted against the last rays of the setting sun. The heavens exploded in a cataclysmic confrontation, churning the chaos awaiting the invaders.

The huge Keeper turned to Dadeus, "I hope this will reinforce the efforts of our friends!"

"We have the advantage of fighting this battle on your island. Having the locals working with *seers* and friends, from all over the planet, gives us an edge. If nothing else, the dueling storms will disrupt their coordination."

"I hope you're right!" replied the giant Keeper, turning back to his instruments.

~

The divers ran through the front door of the fish shop and plunged into the icy waters of the little cove. Long silver bubbles formed around their gleaming suits and they streaked through the mouth of the inlet, fanning out to search north and south. The water was churning with the surge of the approaching squall driving most of the smaller sea-creatures deep, seeking shelter out of harms way. Pods of dolphins and whales formed a defensive array of scouts. Morgan headed to the south and was the first to spot two mini-subs approaching the harbor at high speed. "We've got subs headed right for the cove!"

Raffe called into his headset, "Break into two groups. Mary you take Josh and Ian to the sub on the left. We'll take the other one. Grab seagrasses, trash, whatever you can find to stuff into the intakes."

Morgan, Molly, and Megan formed up with Raffe, while Josh and Ian took off to the north with Mary. They dove to the bottom, scalping debris, kelp, and grasses, before intercepting the submarines a half-mile off shore.

Intakes inhaled seawater on either side of the bow into jets that propelled the subs at astonishing speeds. The teams stuffed everything that they could find into the ports and the little vessels slowed to a crawl. The divers gathered on the skins of the sleek crafts and waited. After a few moments, the hatches opened and the first divers in dry suits began to emerge.

Raffe called, "Shields open and FIRE!"

Molly, Megan, and Morgan opened their protective shields and fired blasts from their rings. The dark troops tried to retreat but Raffe swam over the stern of the first sub and dropped two of the Professor's flash pans into the opening. The blasts blew off the cover and the tiny craft descended to the bottom in a cloud of bubbles. Mary, Josh, and Ian repeated the assault on the second sub, which plunged into the darkness below.

Ian's voice crackled through the headsets, "If there are two, there are more!"

"I know you're right," replied Raffe. "Let's break up. You guys check the harbor north of the mountain and we'll head south. I'm guessing they didn't have time to call their comrades. They won't know that we're waiting for them."

"We're on it," said Mary, joining up with Ian and Josh to cruise north along the coast with Spot, Dusty, and three orcas.

~

The two storms collided over the ridge in a cataclysmic clash, just as the dark warriors split north and south. The ravens strained to maneuver through battering winds raging across the island that swirled into tornadoes dancing through the fields. Tight disciplined formations shattered and small groups struggled for cover.

The first wave of troops emerged from the dueling squalls into a small patch of light illuminating a tall black woman in a long purple dress, carrying a bright red parasol on her shoulder and strolling along the waterfront with a crocodile on a diamond studded leash. A man, dressed in a black suit, with a bowler hat, walked with a briefcase in one hand and a lion tethered to the other. Two older women, with funny little hats balanced on snow white hair, stood on the backs of prancing zebras and several Asian men rode giraffes, loping along a path across the plain. Two American Indians whooped and hollered from the backs of charging bison, followed by a small herd of elephants sauntering along unattended. Dolphins, sharks, and several small whales performed a strange water ballet in the center of the cove, to the delight of a small group of spectators gathered on the quay, disguised as circus performers clapping and cheering with sheer abandon.

Loud marching music blared from the open windows of the shops and large strobe lights flashed with an intensity that rivaled brilliant sunshine.

Disoriented by the music, bright blinking lights, and the strange crowd assembled around the cove, the leader of the attackers reached for his *messenger* to call Zepallo. In that instant, the *seers* transformed and joined local citizens, to aim and fire blasts from rings on their hands and long, slender crystalline hand-cannons. Sixteen of the flying troops were blown from the air. The others turned south and retreated back into the squall.

~

Airborne scouts flew north along the eastern coast and found no obvious defenses, other than a farmer and two field hands shepherding a large herd of cows from one pasture to another through the storm. The leader waved his hand to ignore them and continue to their target, the House of the Four Seasons, on a bluff jutting from the forest climbing the ridge just coming into view through rain and fog.

Sammy and the field hands lifted their hands to the brims of their hats, to signal their hidden comrades, who fired a salvo of blasts from the crystal cannons buried in haystacks, barns, and crooks in the ridge at the passing flock of ravens. Some of the cows transformed into yellow-robed *seers*, who joined in the volley. The tight formation was scattered as fifteen or twenty attackers crashed to the ground. The survivors banked east, into the fury of dueling tornadoes thrashing over the open fields.

Zepallo hovered over the ridge just to the north of the old schoolhouse, surveying his troops in complete disarray. He raised the *messenger* on his wrist to his mouth, "Send in the second and third waves! They are far better prepared than we might have guessed!"

Ptolemy and Wonac were stationed in a mini-sub hovering at one hundred feet, a half-mile east of the crescent beach. Technicians monitored and directed the movements of the troops at banks of communications gear lining the inside of the hull of the little ship, as Ptolemy paced back and forth, shouting, "I knew it was a trap! That fool will be the death of me!"

Ignoring his leader, Wonac maintained a professional calm and spoke quietly into a headset, "Send in the second wave but hold the third, until we have advanced inland. Those who survived the initial assault, regroup at vector point seven and drop in from the north to attack the facilities in the mountain. Exterminate anything that moves!"

Within moments, the skies over the island filled with hundreds of black ravens soaring at top speed through the tempest to their targets.

The human cannon, near the circus tent, swiveled on its base and Travis fired a huge blast of shrapnel at a wave of attackers heading for the observatory. Thirty or forty plummeted into sodden fields. The tent fabric peeled away to reveal a half-dozen cannons, each defending a different section of the sky over the island. Circus performers, who had been milling about the grounds, ran to their stations and fired a torrent of charges at approaching columns of black-cloaked troops.

∼

Nanchez scanned the movements on a *messenger* and cackled into a headset, "They're headed your way, Professor. It's time for the energy shield!"

Ponte grinned, as he watched waves of Dark Forces being dissected by the forces on the ground. "I'm on it!" he shouted, punching a button that raised an energy curtain to surround the observatory. "That should confound them! I think it's time for you *seers* to head out! Watch out for the shield. Remember, you can go under but not over!"

Without a word, Alius, Sky, Master Chi, and Simian flew through the front door to join in the fray.

∼

A wave of airborne troops swarmed to attack the House of the Four Seasons, unaware of Kelly and Dr. Stevens hiding in the woods, up the hill from the old farmhouse, with two-dozen *seers* and a wild herd of animals.

Kelly fingered the watch hanging from a golden chain around her neck, "Dr. Stevens, I have a question."

The Doctor glanced at the youngster, "Which is?"

"Master Chi noticed this watch and said it was a 'turnabout'. What did he mean?"

"Well, as I told you, it is a very special watch. It was handed down through my family and, to tell you the truth, I honestly don't know how old it is, certainly many generations. A turnabout is a timepiece that can manipulate time. By resetting it, it's possible to be in two places at the same time. Actually, it just allows you to repeat time or to move ahead in time. I hate to admit that I used it in school to take two classes during the same hour."

"So, if I didn't like the way something came out, I could go back and relive it?"

"Yes."

"Would I know that I had already been through that time?"

"Yes, you would. You'd have a memory of both experiences but no one else would."

"Does it affect everyone or just the person who's wearing it?"

"Just the person who's wearing it and…anyone they're touching."

"Wow!" Her face lit up in that beautiful smile. "No wonder you told me to be careful with it. You'll have to show me how it works."

"I'll be happy to but I think there might be a better time."

"We could race ahead and see what's going to happen!"

"But we might tip our hand to the Dark Forces and we can't allow that to happen."

"I know you're right," smiled Kelly, "and I hope we don't need it." Turning from the watch, she gazed through driving rain to spot squads of dark uniforms charging across the island.

The headset crackled, "They're headed your way!"

The doctor grabbed Kelly's hand, partly for his own sense of security, at the sound of Brandy barking in the distance. "Hold on, we don't want to move until they reach the fields south of the house!"

"I know!" squeaked Kelly, as she raised her hand above her head. She turned to the herd around her, "Go on my signal!"

The *seers,* citizens of the island, and animals nodded, while the strange little people with the funny hats giggled and laughed.

Ravens soared across the fields from the southeast and attempted to land, as Kelly dropped her hand and a throng of *seers* shot into the air. A barrage of blasts caught the troopers dismounting from their grounded ravens. Civilians and animals charged down the hill, trapping the dark warriors in hand-to-hand combat in the mud with no means of escape.

A swarm of soaring *seers* attacked a squadron of ravens flying cover above the old farmhouse. Thousands of birds swooped just above their black wings, disrupting the airflow and tearing at their feathers as they passed.

Armed with heavy blasters, the dark warriors fired rapid bursts, while Dadeus' rings and hand-cannons required a few moments to recharge. They wore golden shields on their left wrists that opened like shimmering umbrellas, to deflect incoming concussions fired from hordes of ravens, streaking through the tumbling clouds. The youngsters frustrated the seasoned troops, twirling and flipping from one trajectory to another, firing blasts from every angle.

The animals and people from the island descended from the forest and formed a cordon around the House of the Four Seasons, swelling to contain each advancing throng. Brandy led the movements and Tic acted as a spotter from his perch on top of the barn. The defense was holding for the moment but John was detaining the animals from the plane, until the next wave arrived.

∿

From their perch on the ridge just to the south of the school, Adrian could see the flashes of charges exploding and sensed the struggle rolling across the island. The novice eagle flapped his wings, as an electric spike tore up his spine into the base of his skull. Zepallo was nearby.

Magnus cautioned, "Wait. Our time is coming. Just a few moments more!"

"I can feel Zepallo and he's close by!"

"All the more reason to be patient," replied the beautiful eagle in a calm quiet voice. "We know that they'll have staggered waves of troops and we don't want to be caught between them. We want to trap them all!"

Ruffling his feathers impatiently, Adrian felt a massive disruption in the energies and knew that the reinforcements were moving into the battle. "It's time. Let's go," he shouted to the animals hiding in the forest along the ridge.

The immense horde slipped through the vent and charged out of the woods and across the meadow towards the House of the Four Seasons to join in the battle. One contingent of the menagerie swept north to defend the observatory and the mountain, while another herd rumbled through muddy fields to trap a squadron of dark warriors advancing on the little village.

~

The Dark Forces bombarded the energy shield around Ponte's home with an incessant barrage of purple charges and flew erratic ellipses, searching for a seam or a gap. Thousands of birds swarmed regimented flights of ravens, swooping close to their wings to break the flow of air holding them aloft. A half-dozen pterodactyls swooped out of churning clouds to protect the dark riders, their long wings sweeping through the storm in long graceful arcs and open beaks shrieking a deafening chirping cry that terrified humans and animals alike.

Alius, Sky, Master Chi, and a half-dozen other *seers* attacked a squadron of ravens circling just outside the shield. Alius secretly wished that she had spent a bit more time practicing the art of levitating, as she tumbled through the air, dodging blasts from the bad guys. The *seers* formed a circle, accelerating around the shield at an incredible rate in the opposite direction as the riders were flying. Before the dark warriors could aim at an approaching *seer*, another was firing at them from behind. The effect was devastating.

Sammy and the Keepers directed cannons in well-concealed niches along the ridge, creating overlapping target cones, and fired repeated blasts, ravaging waves of invaders closing on the observatory and the old farmhouse. The little people from South America devised a cannon shot of thin golden nets that flew a great distance before discharging a web to swallow flocks of ravens and their riders in a tangle.

Kelly and Dr. Stevens, hidden in the forest above the House of the Four Seasons, watched Adrian and Magnus soar out of the trees into a long slow arc over the fields, dropping over the bluff to the east, around to the south to climb the thermals from Nanchez' squall above the ridge. The eagles joined a cloud of hundreds of birds, brilliant colors swirling through gray chaos, chasing a black blur of ravens struggling through clashing storms.

Everywhere he looked in the air and on the ground, *seers* and animals were isolating and attacking the Dark Forces. Waves of animals roared out of the woods into the fracas around the old farmhouse to drive the enemy across the eastern plain. On the bluff overlooking their favorite beach, he spied a dragon climbing the stone steps flaring long tongues of fire from his snout. A monster sure to bolster Zepallo's desperate troops, who were retreating ahead of a massive surge of lions, tigers, and panthers charging into the throng, followed closely by packs of dogs, wolves, coyote, and fox, backed by elephants, hippopotamus, bison, wildebeest, several bears, gorillas, and an incredible collection of friends.

As they passed over the bluff, Adrian looked down along the coast at a creeping checkerboard of shadows in the shallows of the surf where sharks, dolphins, whales, and enormous schools of other fish waited for any invaders foolish enough to attempt to breach their barrier. A giant blast erupted from the ocean a half-mile offshore, sure sign that his friends destroyed another mini-sub.

The eagles led a patchwork of vibrant wings flapping through clashing winds and sheets of rain, frozen in space by fierce lightning. They crested the ridge from the southwest, rising high on storm winds to spot Zepallo, surrounded by several dozen of his elite troops, hovering a hundred feet above the schoolyard. Adrian's enemy was presiding over battles, raging across the island, and directing his troops, like the generals of great armies in times long since passed.

Waves of ravens swooped in from the east to reinforce desperate pockets of warriors brawling around the farmhouse, in the village, just outside the shield at the observatory, at both entrances to the mountain, and across the fields to the ocean.

In a flash, he understood that success in defending the island depended on disrupting the coordination Zepallo was supplying to his troops. This moment was preordained by their skirmishes in Peru, New York, here on Morgan's Knot, and on the dock of his boyhood home. He paused to summon the images the Dark Lord presented on that dark night…his aging mother, his own death, and the raging fire crawling across the island. The only prophesy that seemed possible was that he might die in this coming confrontation with the Dark Lord. The ground was too wet for a wildfire and his mother was not yet an old woman, *"I know he invented two of the three horrors he predicted. I'm willing to bet the third one was a mirage too!"*

Everything around him vanished…the din of the storms boiling overhead, battles raging all over the island, tracers streaking through the torrent to explode in violent flashes faded into white noise. Each explosion threatened so many of his friends and family toiling to defend the future of the Balance. Adrian's focus zeroed in on the Dark Lord and the prickly blue static sparking in the cold dark luster of his aura, as he hovered on a giant raven below the young *seer*.

Zepallo spun around to scan the sky, just as Adrian winked at Magnus, tucked his wings close to his body, and dropped straight down at an astonishing speed.

~

John, Brandy, Tic, and their comrades cheered the animals charging down the hill to battle swarms of black-caped warriors slogging through soggy fields. The animals of the island, local residents, and a few dozen *seers* managed to stymie the first two waves but he knew they would be hard-pressed to repel the next onslaught.

A relentless attack by lions, saber-toothed tigers, panthers, elephants, herds of bison, bears, boar, wolves, and hundreds of other animals herded several dragons, spewing plumes of orange flames in defense of the ranks of invaders, off the bluffs. Animals and *seers* surrounded huge blotches of black uniforms, a voracious amoeba apportioning them into smaller and smaller islands of obstructed isolation. The tide of this battle was shifting and John prayed his friends and family were finding similar success, as he released another onslaught of animals into the melee.

~

Nanchez and Dadeus worked furiously to maintain the storm over the island, drawing maximum energy from the Black Crystal, because Ponte confiscated the vectors of the Golden Crystal to power the energy shield and the crystal cannons.

Messengers burst into the workshop every few minutes to update the battle raging outside the northern entrance and the harbor. The Dark Forces were having a hard time getting close to the tunnels through heavy resistance by the *Others'* sentries and a flight of *seers* defending the mountain. The most recent missive reported that a large group of animals from the plane dropped out of the vent and was driving the enemy north along the coast towards the circus fortifications.

~

Morgan, Raffe, Molly, and Megan, along with a pod of dolphins and whales, found two more mini-subs and dispatched them to the bottom. The cheers and chatter in their headsets, from Mary, Josh, and Ian, confirmed the destruction of two submarines in the mouth of the tiny cove outside the entrance to the tunnels.

Somehow, the mountain seemed an obvious primary objective but Morgan was confident the disciplined people, now her people, manning the chambers within the black rock, would deny the invading troops any opportunity to seize control of the Black Crystal.

Her escort of two dolphins stopped and pointed to the east. Their tails swayed back and forth in a slow considered rhythm, as they focused their sonar on a distant target. Suddenly, their tails fluttered and both started clicking, indicating a single sub, this one farther from shore than the rest.

She whispered into her mouthpiece, "I wonder whether this might be their command center? All of the others have been patrolling in pairs."

Raffe's voice was very calm, pointing to the whales and dolphins, "I think you might be on to something. These guys are headed in a straight line and I'd guess the target isn't moving."

Two whales raced out ahead of the group and swam to either side of a sleek black submarine hovering in the dark waters one hundred feet beneath the surface. The two giants of the sea gracefully turned and pulled up next to the sub, inching into the sides of the craft to crush against the hull, heavy blubber folding over the intakes to erase any hope of propulsion. With a deep raucous rumble and a flip of their tails, they slammed the black sub to the bottom, crashing it nose first into a rocky outcrop in a cloud of bubbles.

~

George's voice was anxious, "How's it going at the observatory?"

The Professor laughed, "The energy shield is secure and our *seers* are zipping around the tower like whirling dervishes! So far, we're holding our own!"

"Good," replied George, "We've driven off wave after wave of ravens but enough of them landed to attack on two fronts. Fortunately, the animals appeared at just the right moment. Their formations have been divided and forced into retreat. Has anyone heard from Adrian?"

"No. We haven't had any communication but, then, he doesn't have a headset. Raffe radioed in to say they think they sank a command sub. That should slow them down!"

"That's grand," replied George, firing another round from the crystal cannon at a swarm of ravens approaching from the south. "Sorry about the racket. I'll get back to you."

Flocks of ravens plunged into the scuffle to cover a wretched straggle of warriors retreating south, while waves of animals and *seers* in circus costumes funneled squadrons of invaders out into the fields, away from the village, under a barrage of fire from a battery of crystal cannons mounted on floating go-carts. Although, there was considerable damage, the little shops and the funhouse might survive.

~

Zepallo touched his earpiece and raised the *messenger* to his mouth, "Command Center! We're facing a counter-attack. Airborne troops regroup to strike the observatory on the column of rock. I will deal with our primary target!"

Unintelligible voices crackled through roaring static in response. He nudged the giant raven into flight and turned, just as Adrian streaked out of furious clouds with the precision of an aerial predator, followed by a flock of screeching birds.

The young *seer* morphed into his human form and drew the sword from beneath his robes, pressing the blue crystal to extend a gleaming golden shaft from the handle. Blinded by crashing pain at the base of his skull, he lost track of the birds diving out of the sky to overwhelm the contingent guarding the Dark Lord. A curious smile in Zepallo's eyes locked into perfect focus, as the giant raven banked to meet the attack.

Everything slowed, as the Evil One raised his hand and fired a blast at the human meteor rushing out of the storm. Adrian dodged to his left and pressed the red crystal on the hilt, discharging a mighty bolt of lightning that struck one of the raven riders flying next to his target. A cloud of black feathers trailed the enormous bird, as it fluttered through the trees and tumbled down the ridge.

Adrian raised the gleaming blade to swing at Zepallo as he streaked past, grazing his swirling black cape. He twirled around, opened the shield on his wrist, and soared at his enemy. Too engrossed in his duel to notice, other birds transformed into tall black *seers* to engage the Dark Lord's shock troops, while the rest dispersed fleeing flocks of ravens.

Zepallo turned to confront the young *seer* and fired another blast from his ring. The energy careened off the golden shield with a mighty 'clang', spinning the boy into a corkscrew diving directly at his adversary. He pressed the red crystal on the handle of his sword and a bolt clipped the wingtip of the raven carrying the Dark Lord. The huge black bird dipped to the right, just as Adrian swooped past, swinging his sword with all his might. He grazed Zepallo's leg and nipped the tail-feathers of the raven, which screeched and flapped desperately to maintain a long slow spiral into the forest.

The Dark Lord leapt from the giant bird in mid-air and spun to face his young adversary. His wet hair thrashed around cold blue eyes in a pallid face and his dark robes glimmered in the flicker of lightning striking a tree at the base of the ridge. In that moment, Adrian could see the dogged intensity in Zepallo's eyes, as he reached with one hand to touch the wound on his leg and drew a black sword from beneath his cloak with the other.

The Evil One soared through the air with practiced grace and speed, firing a mighty blast that glanced off Adrian's shield, thumping him into a backwards tumble. The boy extended his arms and legs and flipped over to raise his sword to deflect a brutal blow, as Zepallo flew past in a blur.

Sparks exploded as glowing blades clashed in a shower of magenta and golden embers, their bodies hurled into orbit around each other in the very core of the clashing storms. Flitting through the clouds like a human hummingbird, Adrian managed to dodge blows from the gleaming black sword and sensed Zepallo's frustration. The Dark Master's size, strength, and skill were honed and lethal but no match for the speed and agility of his young foe. Thunder rattled across the island, as hundreds of lightning flashes strobed their movements into an old-time movie.

The battles raging across the eastern range slowly ebbed, as combatants turned to gape in astonishment, realizing that the outcome of the siege would be determined by the victor in the furious clash in the clouds.

Each time Zepallo struck a blow, the dark warriors cheered and the Forces of the Light would moan and gasp. When Adrian seemed to take an advantage, the troops in the black robes would curse and the defenders would scream and shout, mere spectators transfixed by a death match between gladiators in the sky.

The two foes flew through torrential rain and buffeting winds to charge each other again and again, until they hovered, silhouetted against continuous curtains of crackling lightning. Zepallo was bleeding from his temple and bore wounds on his hand and his thigh, while Adrian suffered a gash from a charge to his left leg, just above the scar from his battle with Alius on the mountain.

The young *seer* gasped for air. *"If I feel this bad, he's got to feel worse!"* he thought, pressing his sodden robe into the wound on his leg. "Your evil will never overcome the power of the Light!"

Zepallo raised his bleeding hand, his sword extended in the air, the blade a black crystal magnet drawing massive bolts crackling through the heavens. A tight throbbing cloud, sizzling with static, gathered around his rapier and he lowered the tip to the young *seer*. His steely eyes crinkled into an evil sneer, "Tragically, this is the white light that ends your life! Good-bye my young Adrian!"

Time slowed, as Zepallo fired a blistering blast from his sword and panic coursed through the boy's body, as the ball of fire rushed through the storm. Before he could react, the soothing voice of Master Chi chimed in his head, *"At all times, you must remain calm. The outcome of this battle will depend on your ability to focus your mind and your powers. If you truly believe, then no one can defeat you!"*

Adrian retracted his shield and took the sword in both hands, holding it upright in front of his face, while exhaling a long slow breath, calming every cell in his body. He focused on the fireball, a cold electric aura pulsing frantically as it streaked through pelting rain, trailing a shroud of steam and sparks, shimmering the sheen of a comet's blue stardust in its wake. At once, beautiful and terrifying, embodying all of the negative energy on the planet, the young *seer* accepted the magnitude of the moment, where the future of the Powers would be decided.

In slow motion, he drifted to his left, raising the sword behind his shoulder to strike the throbbing sphere with all his might. The blade shattered in a colossal explosion and the shock of the impact convulsed his entire body but he gripped the jewel-studded hilt with both hands.

As the fireball burst with blinding intensity around Adrian, a shaft of blue lightning flashed back at Zepallo, exploding into his chest before he could react. A deep guttural howl filled the air, as he tumbled to the ground and his cloak spread out, like the wings of a wounded bat, around his charred and smoldering body. He stared up at the young *seer,* hanging in the air, pointing the remains of his useless golden sword at the Dark Lord's heart. The defeated *seer* lifted the tips of the fingers of his right hand to his brow and his lips curled into an evil snarl, "I must bow to your powers but this contest has only just begun! Now you and I have a history and my retribution will produce suffering and anguish that will fulfill your worst nightmares!" He tilted his head slightly, transformed into a hissing serpent that fizzled into a curl of black smoke and vanished in the gale.

Adrian tumbled like a rag doll to the spot where his adversary disappeared and crumpled to the ground, as a mighty lightning bolt raced through the sky, illuminating the whole island, followed by a deafening clap of thunder that rumbled out across a ferocious sea.

Before the battle could resume, the troops of the Dark Forces vaporized into puffs of gray mist, just as the storm clouds began to recede. A hearty cheer echoed across the island, as the defenders realized that the opposition had withdrawn.

Panic ravaged John, as he watched the battle in the sky, and ran towards the spot where Adrian crashed into the pasture.

Unis flew up beside him, "Climb on and I'll get you there!"

John leapt onto her back and flew across the trampled field to the south of the House of the Four Seasons. By the time they arrived, Magnus and several *seers* were gathered around a small crumpled heap of tattered blue robes on the ground.

Adrian's father rushed to his son and dropped to his knees. The young *seer* was lying face down and John gently rolled him over, leaning to place his ear near Adrian's mouth. He was breathing.

Within moments, Alius, Master Chi, and Simian arrived, followed by Sky, Mary, and Shambala. Alius ran to her friend, moaning, "Is he alright?" She knelt beside Adrian's father and reached to brush the mud from the boy's face. She felt his breath on her hand, "He's alive!"

Kelly and Dr. Stevens arrived a moment later. Kelly fingered the watch hanging from her neck, wondering whether this might be the moment to turn back time?

The Doctor knelt beside Master Chi on the opposite side of Adrian's body and placed his hand on the young *seer's* chest, "We have a pulse and his breathing is slow and shallow."

"But his aura is strong," added the old master.

Inspecting the unconscious boy, Dr. Stevens touched the wound on his leg. "This needs attention but I think he'll live."

John picked up his son and started to the House of the Four Seasons. The *seers* gathered around and levitated Adrian's body from his father's grasp to float through the air, followed by an incredible procession of animals marching silently across the field. In reverence, they all joined in the universal tone, 'Om'…in long slow waves of hypnotic sound.

Chapter Ten

The gleaming silver crescent of a full moon appeared over a furious ocean, icy light glittering across the crests of massive chaotic waves crashing in all directions, as the storm clouds parted. All of Adrian's friends and family waited on the steps, as the procession arrived at the House of Four Seasons. Sara rushed to John, as the front door opened to allow Adrian's body to float into the house, up the stairs, and onto his bed.

Dr. Stevens leaned over the young *seer* to check his pulse and breathing, before producing a tiny *orb* from his pocket to look into his patient's eyes. He pulled up the blue robes to inspect the burn on Adrian's leg, "That doesn't look good but, with a little attention, it will heal."

People and animals crowded in, as he turned to John and Sara and said, "I think he'll survive. He wasn't fit when he entered this battle and he's exhausted every ounce of energy in his body. I'll fetch some of my healing waters for this wound but, in the meantime, let's get him out of these wet robes and let him rest."

Orbs glowed in the hallway as the crowd retreated from the bedroom, while Sara and Elsie pulled off his ragged robes, washed the dirt and grime from his face and arms, and covered him with blankets. His mother sat on the edge of the bed and touched his cheek, "I am so very proud of you but I'm not sure how often my heart can take the panic I feel when you do these things!"

She leaned over and gently kissed his forehead. Elsie walked over and to rub her sister's shoulders, "You have every right to be proud and scared. He is a very brave young man."

Adrian's mother reached up to her sister and started to cry.

∼

The house full of people paraded after Alius, Master Chi, and little Sky out the front door, greeted by a tremendous cheer from a vast herd of animals and friends, who filled the fields for as far as the eye could see across the eastern plain.

Master Chi linked his arms through those of his fellow *seers* and stepped to the front of the top stair, "My friends! I believe that I speak for everyone who contributed to this battle, when I say 'Thank You' to every one of you for your bravery, your help, and your dedication to the Balance. I doubt that we have truly defeated the Dark Forces but surely we have dealt them a mighty blow and driven them back to their lairs for the time being!"

The crowd roared their approval.

The old *seer* raised chubby hands for quiet, "I must also report that our young *seer*, Adrian, has been injured…but he will live to lead us another day!"

Again, the crowd exploded with cheers and applause.

He turned to inspect the old farmhouse. "I see that the House of the Four Seasons has suffered some damage. Has anyone inspected the rest of the island?"

Professor Ponte stepped to the front, with Ester on his arm, "We've just come from the observatory and it is untouched!"

"Bravo!" shouted Alius.

Alius' father, Jofre, moved to stand beside the Professor, "They managed to sink one of our trawlers but they did no damage to the mountain or our facilities!"

George emerged from the house and pushed to the front, "I can report some damage to the village but we can certainly repair it! My concern is the state of the fields. I'm sure that many will have to be replanted after the deluge and armies tramping through the mud."

Sammy pushed to the front of the crowd, "As I look around at all these friends, I'm sure that you will have all the help that you might need!"

The crowd cheered, as Unis leaned over to nuzzle Sammy, before saying, "I believe it is time for us to leave. Let us all be thankful for each other and our success. We've managed to hand the Evil Ones a defeat and I'm sure that Orana will be proud of all of us!"

Again, the crowd erupted with approval.

"Please give young Adrian our best wishes for a speedy recovery. I'm looking forward to seeing him, when he comes to visit Orana."

Master Chi, Alius, and Sky bowed to the beautiful unicorn. "We are in your debt."

"If our efforts begin the process of healing the Earth, then we all benefit," replied Unis, her golden horn glistened in the light of the *orbs* beside the front door. She turned to lead an endless procession of animals in a massive charge around the barn and up the ridge, where they disappeared.

Most of the animals from the island began to wander away, as Tic and Brandy ran up the steps and into the old farmhouse. The remaining *seers*, Keepers, and neighbors crowded into the house and the festivities lasted until dawn.

~

Adrian awoke to find Alius and Morgan curled up on his bed and Tic and Brandy tangled in a tight furry ball on the floor. Sunlight streamed through the gaps in the curtains billowing from the window, silhouetting his mother asleep in a chair. He rolled onto his back and reached under the covers to touch the bandage covering his throbbing wound. Vigor and vitality had been drained from every muscle in his body and his head was throbbing. The glow of his aura flickered and sputtered…but he was alive, surrounded by those who loved him most.

He smiled to himself, glancing from his mother to the two girls and the pets on the floor, thinking back to the emotions that wracked his mind during his time inside the black *orb* in Zepallo's lair. *"If I had just continued with my studies…if I had just left the Black Book in my pouch…I could have saved her this worry. Tomorrow would have come, just like any other day, and we would all be together."* The fact that he was in his own bed in the House of the Four Seasons meant the Dark Forces had been defeated. *"This is the dawn of a new day!"*

Alius and Morgan stirred, as he shifted, and rolled over to face him, leaning on their elbows to stare at their wounded friend. "It's nice to see that you're going to survive," joked Morgan.

Alius snickered, "We had our doubts!"

"What happened?"

"Before or after your drove Zepallo into the ground?" smiled Morgan, as Sara roused and reached for her son.

"I don't remember much. It was so strange. All I could see was the evil smile on his face and I knew that, one way or another, our future was going to be decided in that instant."

His mother sat up and straightened her skirt, "He fired explosive charges at you. We all watched the pulsing light fly across the sky but you retracted your shield, raised your sword above your head, and swung at the fireball, almost in slow motion. There was a huge flash and a bolt of lightning slammed Zepallo square in the chest and he crashed to the ground. We couldn't see what happened next but you spiraled into the fields like a bird with a broken wing. Your father and the *seers* found you and brought you here."

Adrian smiled and settled back in his pillows. He remembered the look on the Dark Lord's face, as he raised bloody fingertips to his forehead in a mock salute, transformed into a serpent, and disappeared in a puff of smoke. His last words echoed through Adrian's mind, "Now you and I have a history and my retribution will produce suffering and anguish that will fulfill your worst nightmares!"

"We're not finished with him," sighed the young *seer*, "but we handed him a monumental defeat. It will take time for them to repair the damage and rebuild their losses."

Sara moaned, "Maybe things will calm down around here for a change!"

Morgan laughed, "You missed a great party!"

"Yeah, it was probably the biggest gathering this house has ever seen!" smiled Alius. "The animals from the plane left last night but most of the *seers* and Keepers are going to stick around for a few days to help with the repairs and to consult with Ponte, Nanchez, and Dadeus. I think they all enjoy the opportunity to work with their peers!"

Adrian laughed, "Do they all talk like Nanchez and Ponte, when they get into their weird science dialect of speaking in little fragments that make no sense to anyone else?"

Alius started giggling, "No, some of them actually talk in complete sentences and ten or twelve languages! I was completely intimidated, when I had to get all of them to stop jabbering and start building the defenses! At first, they all looked at me, as if I were some stupid little blond girl, who didn't know anything. I fixed that!"

"I'll bet you did!" smirked Adrian. "You don't hold much back."

Tic jumped up onto the bed and walked across Adrian's chest to lick his nose, "I'm glad to see you're back with us!"

Brandy rested his nose on the edge of the bed, looking for a pet.

"As always, we have the two of you to thank for all of your help."

Brandy tilted his head, "As far as we're concerned, we're all in this together."

"We're all very thankful for what you've accomplished but, just make sure that you stay humble, if you weren't injured we'd beat you up!" added Morgan, reaching to tickle him under his ribs.

Sara rose from her chair, "I'm for that! Now, why don't you ladies go find out what's for breakfast, for humans and the animals, while I clean up this young hero a little."

Adrian grabbed Alius' hand, "I want to thank you. We won this battle because you organized our forces and made it all work to our advantage. Without you, I'd be dead and Morgan's Knot wouldn't exist."

Alius blushed, "To tell you the truth, I spent a lot of time thinking about how you would find a solution to the challenge we were facing. In hindsight, I think we would have fought to a draw with the

Dark Forces but, it all came down to the fact that, this was all about a personal war between you and Zepallo. We were lucky. We won this battle…and we were victorious because you defeated the Dark Lord."

Adrian pursed his lips, "I wouldn't have had the opportunity or the advantage without you and all you accomplished. You're amazing."

"As you always say, I just did what had to be done and you would have done the same things."

"That does sound familiar," groaned the wounded *seer*.

The two girls kissed him on the forehead and wandered out of the room, as Sara sat on the edge of the bed and brushed tangled hair from his brow, "I have to say that I am very proud of you but I also must add that I'm panic stricken when you face these dangers."

"I know and I wish I could pass my responsibilities off to someone else but we both know I can't. Did they tell you that Orana wants me to spend some time with her?"

Sara sighed, "I know but you're not going anywhere until you've recovered fully. I think I'm entitled, as your mother, to demand that you stay put until then."

"I agree," smiled Adrian, as she walked over to the bathroom and returned with a warm washcloth to wipe his face.

"Now, how do you feel?"

"I feel…as if I've been in a brawl with a very tough grownup *seer*, who beat me soundly!"

"Good," laughed his mother. "Maybe you'll do as your told for a change!"

"I promise!"

"How's the wound on your leg?"

"It's sore and it throbs but it could be worse."

"That might be because Dr. Stevens cleaned the wound with his healing waters. He said that he'd come back to check on you this morning."

"He and I have to stop meeting like this!"

"I'll second that! Now you stay put and I'll go see whether Elsie and the girls are making some breakfast for you."

Adrian eased back onto his pillows, "I'm hungry!"

Suddenly serious, he looked up at his mother, "How bad were our losses?"

"There are quite a few people in the infirmary, as well as a fair number of animals, most with burns from the dragons, but, all in all, we were lucky. No one died. The strangest thing was that all the fallen troops of the Dark Forces disappeared when they withdrew. We don't know how many of them were killed or injured."

"That doesn't surprise me," replied Adrian softly. "They don't want us to know."

"I guess we'll never have any way to comprehend the full extent of this victory. Perhaps we should be grateful that we survived."

"We won the battle but not the war. It would be foolish to think we're finished. As long as Zepallo is alive and there is a Legio Obscurum, this struggle will continue. We just don't know where or when."

"I'm afraid you're probably right," said his mother, a tear trickled from the sadness in her exhausted eyes. "We were fortunate to have all the help from the *seers*, the Keepers, and the animals from the plane. One of these times, Zepallo will find you alone and that frightens me."

"It's funny but I don't think he can defeat me. During our fight, I just knew in my heart that he couldn't win. The Light is stronger than the Dark and maybe that's the simple answer to the challenge. As long as I believe, he'll never defeat me."

Sara leaned over and kissed her son's forehead, "I pray that you're right."

Without another word, she turned and marched out the door to hide her tears.

~

A week after the battle, repairs to the House of the Four Seasons and the little village were nearing completion. The roof and walls of the old house suffered several blasts and the old barn was scorched and scarred.

Seers levitated pallets of shingles onto the roof from a parade of trolleys, as Adrian emerged into the sunshine for the first time since the invasion. He gazed around at the bustling activity, until his eyes scanned across the trampled fields, astonished at the extent of the damage the troops and animals had inflicted on the crops.

Farm animals pulled plows to smooth and furrow the earth and hundreds of crouching volunteers planted seeds and shoots.

All of the children gathered around the young *seer*, as Raffe wrapped an arm around his shoulders, "I heard you had a little tussle with Zepallo! You should have been with us, we blew up at least six of their subs and the whales rammed their command center into the bottom. It was spectacular!"

"I have no doubt," replied Adrian. "How's the little village?"

"Travis and my dad are working on the repairs with a lot of the local people, several *seers*, and a few Keepers. At least they didn't get to the funhouse!" laughed Megan.

Brandy and Tic loped up to the group, as Adrian hobbled over to the vegetable garden on a single crutch. "Hey, you two! I can't thank you enough for your help in the battle!"

Brandy rubbed against his good leg and wagged his tail, "It was good fun! Those bad guys were fearless but I got a taste of a few of them!"

"We couldn't have won without you and the other animals."

"Did anyone tell you that all of the fighting on the island stopped when you and Zepallo started your duel?"

Adrian stared at the dog, without really comprehending, "You're kidding?"

"No, I'm not. It was like a very strange sport, where the spectators fought with each other until the main event commenced, then each side cheered on their warrior and cursed any advantage for the opposition. As soon as the outcome was determined and Zepallo fell out of the sky, all of the troops of the Dark Forces disappeared and all of their wounded and dead vanished with them."

"That's amazing!" smiled Adrian, as he reached down to pet the red dog behind the ears, "I sure am thankful for the two of you!"

Tic rubbed up against his ankle and purred.

~

By the time Adrian recovered enough to walk without a cane, the fields were swathed under an electric-green blanket of new sprouts. Alius and Morgan joined him each afternoon for a hobble along the paths between the pastures to exercise his leg and to get him out of the house. He had yet to return to school but he waded through his assignments for several hours each day.

A cold gusty wind blew in off the ocean but deep blue sky followed an orange sun sinking into the top of the ridge, as they turned into the yard of the House of the Four Seasons. "When are you coming back to school?" inquired Morgan, as they walked into the shadow of the house.

"I'm not sure that I'll be back for a while," replied Adrian. "I got a message from Sky that Orana is looking forward to seeing me. I got the impression that I was expected sooner rather than later."

"I wish I could go with you," moaned Alius. "She's an incredible woman and I'd give anything for a chance to train with her."

"I'll ask her whether she'd consider taking on a couple of additional students!"

"Oh, that would be so great!"

"Now, I'm becoming jealous of the two of you!" laughed Morgan. "I've always been envious of your powers and your knowledge about the secrets."

Adrian hugged her, "We've learned that at least some of these powers are available to everyone, we just haven't figured out how to teach people, who aren't *seers*, to levitate or ride the vectors. That's something I want to ask Orana about."

Morgan laughed, "Well, I'm first in line, after you get to talk with her!"

The two girls wrapped their arms under Adrian's and the trio climbed the steps into the House of the Four Seasons.

~

Sky and Master Chi materialized in front of the vegetable garden, which was overflowing with growth. The sun was high in the east and the air crisp and quiet on this cold winter morning.

Adrian opened the front door and staggered down the steps to meet his fellow *seers*, with a noticeable limp and a little help from the twins. He carried a small bag with a few clothes and his most precious possessions.

George, Elsie, John, and Sara followed, as he shuffled over to the garden.

"I want to thank you for coming to escort me to Orana," said Adrian, as he hugged the tiny *seer* and the rotund Master.

Master Chi bowed, "It is a pleasure to see that you are recovering from your battle wounds and both of us are more than happy to guide you." Turning to the adults, he smiled, "He will be in the best of hands."

Sara walked over and hugged Adrian from behind, "This might be the first time that he's gone off on a mission, when I'm not in a panic!"

The young *seer* turned to hug his mother, then his father, his aunt and uncle, and the twins, "I'll see you soon!"

John smiled down at his son, "I'd suggest you pay attention but I don't think there's any doubt about your focus!"

"Promise," smiled Adrian, as he turned to his fellow *seers*, who joined hands and disappeared.

George laughed, "If you thought that he'd grown and matured, when we came to find you on the Island of the Children, the change will be even more dramatic this time!"

Sara wiped the tears from her eyes with the back of her hand, "I know he's got to go but I'm not sure that I'm ready for him to change that much."

John wrapped an arm around her waist, "He has to grow up sometime and he's way ahead of his age as it is…we can't stand in his way."

"I know…but I don't have to like it."

Chapter Eleven

The trio landed in the meadow of the unicorns and found Unis waiting. They walked over to greet her and the other members of her family. "It's so nice to see you!"

"And we're happy to have you here," replied the beautiful unicorn. "Orana has been impatient, anxiously expecting this young man to appear at any moment."

Master Chi laughed, "We all understand that she knows exactly what's going on at all times…everywhere. I'm sure that she knew we were coming, long before we arrived!"

Turning to Adrian, he asked quietly, "Do you remember what I told you before the battle on Morgan's Knot?"

Adrian smiled, "It came to me at the moment when I knew that everything was about to be decided. 'At all times, you must remain calm. The outcome of this battle will depend on your ability to focus your mind and your powers. If you truly believe, then no one can defeat you!'"

The old Master smiled, "I'm pleased that you found my advice useful. This time the enemy will not be Zepallo. On this journey, the enemy will be the demons residing in your soul but, if you truly believe, then no one, including yourself, can defeat you or deny your destiny."

Adrian did not really understand the depth or true meaning in the old *seer's* counsel but he memorized the words and accepted the sincerity in his eyes, with a bow, "Thank you. I'll take your words to heart."

Unis looked at Adrian, "Are you ready?"

"Oh, yes," blushed the young *seer*, turning to hug Master Chi and then Sky.

"I wish I could go with you," whispered Sky, hugging him a moment longer than normal. "You know I'm jealous!"

"I know and I'll ask her about that, when I have a chance," smiled Adrian, limping away to follow Unis up the path.

~

After a short levitation and a long painful climb, they came to the mouth of a large cave. Try as he might, Unis would not answer his questions about Orana or her history. Her only comment, "She will teach you the things that you need to know."

Adrian hugged the unicorn, "Thank you for guiding me."

"It is my pleasure. Now, work hard, because all of us, in all of the planes, are depending on you."

The blond boy smiled, "Lately, it seems, it is I who have been depending on all of you!"

"And that is as it should be…now go on," laughed Unis, nudging him towards the mouth of the cave with her muzzle.

Adrian edged into the darkness and noticed the echo of birds singing an enchanting song and the scent of burning pinion wood. After several twists in the tunnel, he ducked under an intricate spider web to enter a large cavern with the stars of the evening sky shimmering in the ceiling and the familiar emblem glowing on a wall. Flames leapt through un-scorched logs stacked in a fire pit carved into the floor of the cave, and shafts of light streamed through the haze to illuminate an ancient wrinkled woman, hovering a foot above a large smooth stone covered with a thick blanket.

Long white hair, shimmering with the sheen of fine silk, and paisley robes veiled a crooked emaciated body but twinkling eyes delved into his spirit with absolute focus. Adrian did not have to squint to see the powerful pink aura, a glowing cloud surrounding her tiny frame.

A small smile crept across her lips, as she touched the fingertips of each hand together and bowed her head slightly. "I am Orana and it is a pleasure to meet you, young Adrian. I've heard so much about you!" cackled the ancient woman. "If I owned a watch, I would complain that you are tardy!"

Adrian blushed, deciding that any excuse to her last comment would be inadequate, and walked over to squat awkwardly on the opposite side of the fire. "I think that the pleasure should be mine. My friends have told me a little about you and the history of your powers but I'm afraid that I don't know as much as I should."

"Young Sky thinks that you are the 'one,' just as I was the 'one' in my time," mused the old woman. "If that is true, then we probably know more about each other than either of us is willing to admit, for the moment."

Adrian could feel her aura wrapping around his body, warm and secure. "I am the student, you are the Master."

"I'm told that you did not know that you were a *seer*. Is this true?"

"Yes, it is. I was born on the mainland. My mother was from Morgan's Knot but she never told me that she was the daughter of a *seer*, let alone what a *seer* was. She married my father, who was in the Navy before he worked for a firm that designed ships, until they moved his job to Vancouver. I was left on Morgan's Knot for the summer, while they sailed our boat around to the Pacific. When a freak storm came up, there were no *seers* on the island and I was tested."

"And you found that you could read from the Texts! What else did you find?"

Adrian thought for a moment. He felt inept but decided that he would give honest answers to her questions, while leaving out the details, until he understood how her mind worked. "I've learned many things and I'm beginning to master some of my powers but the one thing that stands out in my mind is something that Tic, the cat, told me at the very beginning. He said that understanding is demanding. What he meant was that once someone takes on the responsibility of being a *seer*, they can never give it back, they can never shrink from that obligation, and they must defend the Balance with their lives."

"I think you've got the gist of it," smiled Orana, slowly descending to sit cross-legged on the stone. She leaned to pour two cups of tea from a silver tea service that materialized beside her, "Do you take cream or sugar?"

"A little sugar, please" replied Adrian, reaching to take the delicate cup from her steady, boney hand. The first sip rippled through his body like lapping waves at low tide. His vision blurred for a moment and then cleared to crisp focus, as his senses opened to the power of this woman and the magnitude of her knowledge.

"I had the opposite experience. I always knew that I was a *seer*. Everyone in our family had powers of one sort or another. My father made us read from the Books by candlelight in a root cellar and we were spirited away on the vectors, to meet with other *seers* to learn the secrets from them. In those days, to be accused of being able to read, let alone reading from a forbidden text or believing in the Balance, was a guarantee of a most brutal death."

"There were no countries. Instead, the continent was divided into little fiefdoms, governed by a warlord, his family, allied landowners, a few merchants, and the clergy. They controlled everything...politics, commerce, and religion. If a nobleman coveted for a neighboring city-state, he would send out his armored troops, along with every able-bodied man from the villages, to fight his war. The poor were fodder for his whims, their expendable lives down-payment on expanding his fortune."

"By this point in history, the world had become male dominated. Those, who clung to the beliefs handed down through thousands of years, believed in the equality of all human beings. Men and women held each other in great respect and valued the strengths that each contributed. A woman's opinion was just as valid as a man's and there was...I don't know...a certain courtesy that has been lost." The old woman cackled, "It still makes me mad that we haven't straightened this out in the modern world. Woman are far better equipped for some things than men will ever be!"

Adrian stopped in mid-sip. He was no longer feeling warm and comfortable, realizing that his lessons had begun, "Like what?"

"How about waging war? Men make fierce warriors but most are incapable of becoming true leaders. They lack a certain…ability to see…to comprehend the entire picture. Women are far more open to the world around them. We take in and synthesize everything. We interpret that information with our entire beings, not just our minds! We think with our brains, feel with our hearts, and reach out to touch those around us with our souls. At the same time, we can be utterly ruthless and determined to find the proper path of the correct solution to the problem at hand. Men are far too concerned with the final result, while ignoring the most obvious options."

Adrian pondered her words, "I don't know whether it's my age or, perhaps, my lack of maturity, but I've always heard both male and female voices directing my actions, inside my head."

"Each of us has a little bit of both but our cultures train us to live our lives according to our genders rather than using the best of each. No wonder there are so many confused people in the world. I could never have led the Forces of the Light against our enemies, if our troops had not believed in our equality."

"Tell me about that."

"I was just a little bit older that you are, when the war between the Light and the Dark changed from vigilante guerrilla strikes, by the dark warriors on small groups of *seers*, into a worldwide conflict in the planes. When the battle began, my father charged me with protecting the Books buried in the root cellar. When I felt that it was safe to come out, I found that my entire family had been slaughtered and, somehow, knew that I had been called upon to gather our forces together to lead the fight against our enemies."

"It's strange how you just know," pondered the young *seer*. "No one tells you. No one even asks…it's just the way it is and you do what you must."

The old woman's wrinkled lips curled at the corners, "You do understand."

"There have been times when I've wished that I didn't have these powers."

"That's honest and something that we all feel but we both know that neither of us could walk away from trying to defend the Balance. That, my young charge, is called dedication. In our case, it simply means doing what is required, to the best of our abilities."

Adrian smiled, "I agree."

"Many things have changed in the world, since I was born, but the important things remain the same…love, honesty, bravery, loyalty, and dedication to your cause. Beyond those things, the talents that we inherited and those we develop are merely tools to achieve an end. They are not something to gloat about or to show off to your friends. They're to be nurtured, expanded, and used sparingly," whispered Orana. "The opposite is also true, that evil and hate exist in our world and in our enemies. They will stop at nothing to spread their curse, through the hotspots kindling around the world, to take control of the planet. I led our forces against them many times, just as you have. We were both successful but that does not mean that we are anywhere near finished. They will rise again in one form or another and, now, you will have to be there to stop them."

"There is the other side of all of that. We found it more convenient to work behind the scenes, to avoid the spotlight. The people of the world have enough to worry about and, as you will learn, there are those who would use our powers to their own benefit and that is not what we are about."

"Until your stunt at the United Nations, most of the people of the world had no idea that we or the Balance existed. Now we face two problems. Obviously, the Dark Forces are the most formidable of the two, but now, we have the problem of how to educate our brothers and sisters to cherish the wonders that we must promote and defend."

"On the one hand, we must protect the Crystals and the animal kingdom. On the other, the world would be a better place, if everyone understood and lived by the Balance. It would not surprise me to find that you will become the ambassador for these things. You'll become famous! Crowds will gather when you're in their midst and they'll want to take a little bit of your power with them!

"I already know that sensation," muttered Adrian, "and it's something I suffer rather than cherish."

"Fame will not be your friend. It will be like an itch that you can't scratch or the tiniest splinter buried just beneath the surface of your skin, where you can't relieve the irritation…and it will certainly get in the way of many things that you must accomplish in your lifetime."

"You've succeeded in your battles with the Dark Forces and you're lucky that you're not dead…but then, there are things worse than death!"

Adrian did not know how to respond. He fought his battles with Zepallo and the Dark Forces and he was certain that he would stand against them again. "I am humbled by my success."

"You've been lucky, so far. You don't know what you're doing, even though your sixth sense has guided you to make the right choices at the most critical moments," shouted the old *seer*, waving her hand to release a cloud of blue-green sparkles rising up through the thin plume of smoke from the fire.

"I know you're right but I do have one question, did you know what you were doing, when you led our forces into your first battle all those years ago?"

The old woman doubled over, laughing so hard she clutched her belly, "I think I'm going to like you!"

Her smile drained away, her stare probed into his eyes, into his soul, "There is one more thing that we must discuss before we can proceed and that is the question…have you felt fear?"

Adrian set his teacup on the stone hearth and stared back into her green eyes. This was a moment for honesty. "I've been petrified of the unknown, since I left the mainland. I felt lost and alone, when my parents first abandoned me on Morgan's Knot. I was uncertain when I learned that I could read from the Texts and terrified when I first entered the Golden Crystal. I was hesitant to climb the mountain through a raging blizzard, to change out the balancing crystal, and ill-prepared for my first fight ever…with a girl who had a big knife and bad intentions. I was overwhelmed and desperate, when I thought my parents had been lost in a shipwreck. There have been many times when I have been afraid but, each time, I had no other choice than to continue with what was expected of me. There was no other option."

"What about that scoundrel, Zepallo?" inquired the old woman, her spirit digging into his skull in search of a weakness.

Adrian smiled, "It's kind of funny but I've become less frightened of him, as I've grown to know him as an adversary. Perhaps that's a sign that I'm becoming more confident in my powers but, in our last battle, I knew that he couldn't defeat me. It wasn't that I convinced myself. I just knew in my heart that the Light is more powerful than the Darkness and, no matter what happened, he would not win, even if he killed me."

A small smile curled around Orana's parched lips and her eyes softened, "You've taken a very large step towards your own fulfillment. We all feel fear. If we did not, we would surely allow blind bravery to get in the way of our intelligence and that would lead to our quick demise. No, fear is good but it is something that we must learn to use to our advantage. The chemicals in the body rush to provide energy and focus…being in that peak state, where all of our systems are working together to fight or flee."

"That's exactly how I felt."

"Good. Now you must understand that you were very lucky to have survived engaging someone as skilled and dedicated as the Dark Lord. His level of experience is at the far end of this path that you must travel. He has attained a degree that, for the moment, you can only envy and fear. By all rights, you should be dead."

Adrian blushed and hung his head, whispering, "But I'm not."

"We've learned that at least two of the Master *Seers* for the Dark Forces were killed during the battle on Morgan's Knot. I must assume that they were the only Ministers on the Council who had the strength and stature to balance Zepallo's lust for personal power. Now that they're gone, he will be free to pursue his goals and he'll be far more dangerous than he's been in the past, because he'll have all of the resources and manpower of Legio Obscurum at his disposal. If he did not frighten you in the past, he will the next time you meet…and you will meet again. He is certainly one of the obstacles in the path to your destiny."

The young *seer* suddenly felt cold and began to shiver uncontrollably. The old woman smiled slyly, "As I said, our bodies rush to provide the energy we need, when we go into battle, but it also has the capacity to make us incapable of taking any action…it has the power to render us completely paralyzed and helpless. Learning to control your mind, your body, and your emotions is key to your survival. Something that we'll have to work on, before you will be truly ready to lead the Forces of the Light to defend something as sacred as the Balance."

Adrian stared into her eyes and felt her pink aura reaching out to wrap him in its warmth. Slowly, the trembling subsided and, finally, he took a deep breath to settle himself.

"As you can see, our powers are not confined to fighting our enemies. They touch every part of life and it's important for you to understand that you can and will affect those around you through your strength of will and your self-control. To truly become a *Master Seer*, you must feel everything around you, see the auras and the energies, understand the basic human emotions and motivations that lead people to do the things they do, and to use force only when there really is no other choice." Orana laughed softly, "There will be battles that you will win by doing nothing…by employing restraint, patience, and intelligence to see where your path is leading and understanding the flow of the events unfolding around you."

"It's about seeing, not just what is in front of you but everything and everyone around you…seeing in the present, the past, and the future. It is about seeing truth and there can only be one truth in any situation," lectured Orana. "I'll give you an example. Suppose I were to shuffle a deck of cards and turn them over one by one. Even if you could count the cards and remember what had been played, your chances of predicting each one would be very small, until we got to the end of the pack. On the other hand, a *seer* would know each card before it was turned because there can only be one truth…one possibility that is absolutely correct. That is how we must live our lives. We must know, we must feel, we must see…everything."

"In many ways, the life of a *seer* is very lonely. There's a world that is your reality. It exists beside, but not in, the environment around you. When you're called upon to defend what is right and true, you stand alone by choice. Certainly, others join to fight these battles but you must lead, you must guide your comrades to the correct path, and, when the time comes, you must stand against your enemy. No one else can take your place. No one can shield or protect you. It is your duty to stand between the Light and the Dark."

Adrian nodded his head, "I understand what you're saying. Even though I've had the help of skillful and dedicated *seers* and Keepers, I've always known that it was up to me to lead them into battle and to protect them."

"It would be easier on you, if others were taking these lessons with you but the things that you must learn are unique to you. If I were teaching another student, I would present challenges unique to them. This is a lonely journey that you are about to take, one that will hone your finest qualities and, at the same time, teach you to face your deepest fears and embrace your passions. Are you sure you want to become a *Master Seer*?"

"I believe that is my destiny. I did not choose to become a *seer*. It's just something that I am and I have no other choice than to follow my path and to do my best. There doesn't seem to be any other option."

"There is the choice of returning to your life on the island and remaining the person that you were before."

"I'm trying to learn to be comfortable in my own skin…or, at least, accept my fate. There have been times when I honestly wished that I could just be a normal boy, who grows up to be like his father. Each time I felt that way, fate forced me to take on a new mission and I understood that I could not go back."

Orana smiled, "It is good that you believe in yourself and have a strong spirit, you will need it."

The Cast of Characters

Adrian – son of John and Sara – long and lanky, with blond hair and intense blue eyes

John – Adrian's father – a large man with dark hair and dark eyes, sailor and ship designer

Sara – Adrian's mother – blond, blue eyes, housewife, grew up on Morgan's Knot, daughter of the former *seer*, Paul

George – Adrian's uncle – tall strong, rough hands, salt and pepper hair

Elsie – Adrian's aunt and Sara's sister

Molly and Megan – George & Elsie's twin daughters – blond curly hair blue eyes, a year younger than Adrian

Morgan Keelty – sister of Josh – tall, long curly brown hair, green eyes

Joshua Keelty – Morgan's brother – dark eyes, jet-black hair,

Ian Sheridan – Kelly's brother and Adrian's second cousin – tall, slender

Kelly Sheridan – Ian's younger sister – incredible smile, brown eyes, blond curls

Spot and Dusty – dolphins

Professor Ponte – Keeper of the Powers on Morgan's Knot, astronomer, teacher, and Adrian's mentor

Ester – Ponte's wife - highly intelligent and Ponte's equal

Tic – talking black and white tomcat, Adrian's guide in the animal world

Brandy – Keelty's Irish setter

Travis – harbormaster

Jasmine – Travis' fishing trawler

Dr. Stevens – doctor on the island

Daphne & Dante – deer

Damien – their foal

Beggar – small bear

Magnus – golden eagle

Harriet & Harry – hawks

The Book of Wisdoms – The Golden Book on Morgan's Knot

The Book of Knowledge – The Silver Book used by the *Others* to master the Dark Powers

Jamaica

Simian – Jamaican *seer*, Sammy's uncle

Sammy –Simian's nephew – young Keeper in training

Lorraine – Simian's wife

The *Others*

Alius – daughter of Jofre – the Other's *seer* - petite, blond, blue eyes, tough, independent, and beautiful

Jofre – father of Alius and Master of the *Others* – huge man with white eyes

Mandor – Supervisor of Production and Security – dark eyes, long straight white hair

Nanchez – Keeper of the Dark Powers – a giant of a man with white hair, dark eyes

The Island of the Children

Raffe – young, athletic, and naïve *seer* from The Island of the Children

Gabrielle – leader of the Underworld – Mary's husband, long white hair and beard

Dadeus – Keeper of the Powers for the underworld

Mary – Gabrielle's wife, *seer*

Morag and Jim – Raffe's parents

Book of Natural Balance – The Golden Book on the Island of the Children

Additional Characters

Sky – tiny Thai *seer* – from the Temple of Spiritual Harmony, Thailand

Master Chi – M*aster seer* - Temple of Ancient Truths – Himilayas

Master Jung – slender old Keeper – Temple of Ancient Truths

Mantis – Sky's mentor

Shambala – African *seer*

Mambazi – little girl in Shambala's village

Lala & Maze – *seers* from the southern tip of South America

The Plane of the Animals

Orana – the oldest *seer* on the planet

Unis – female unicorn

Malan – Unis' mate

Legio Obscurum

Zepallo – The Dark Lord – A Minister of Cultural Relations of the Council of Ollapez

Ptolemy – Head of the council – an ancient and domineering dark *seer* and Minister of Internal Affairs with a gray beard

Wonac – Master *seer*, Council member – a hulking Dark Master who presides over the military

Islands of the Mind

Morgan's Knot – A Serial Fantasy
Episode VI

Preview

Adrian was mesmerized by the serene intensity in the ancient *seer's* eyes. Orana's words echoed around the stonewalls of the cave like thunder in the darkness, the tones and syllables reverberating in a strange hypnotic rhythm in his mind, "It is good that you believe in yourself and have a strong spirit, you will need it."

The young *seer* bowed his head, accepting the inadequacy of his powers. In spite of the lessons that allowed him to survive, he was acutely aware that he was a student sitting at the Master's knee and there was little doubt that the imminent instruction would push him beyond anything that he had encountered before, including his skirmishes with Zepallo. Visions of dark caverns and evil creatures crept through his imagination and he struggled to push those images aside.

It was not that he was frightened of the unknown, rather, the anticipation primed him to reach into that well of inner strength that loosed a rush of adrenaline coursing through his system. The hairs on the back of his neck were standing on end and his muscles tensed, ready to spring. All of his senses were open, prepared to collect information, aware of everything around him…the trickling of running water, the emblem on the wall, the birds singing softly, the rhythm of his own breathing and the thumping of his heart beating in his chest, the quiet crackle of the fire, the light streaming through thin pinion smoke in the air, the pink aura surrounding Orana like a bloated feather boa, and the knowing passion in her emerald eyes.

He could feel her energy swaddling him in a warm embrace but her eyes were burrowing into his soul and he knew that it would be impossible to hide anything from this woman.

"Ah, you feel it, don't you?"

Adrian raised his head and met her stare.

"You feel those chemicals churning through your body. Every sense is primed to take in everything around you...sounds, smells, temperature, the movement of the air across your skin, the taste of the tea that lingers on the palette, the texture and rhythm of the energies, and the streams of light flowing into this dark space. If there was movement anywhere close by, you would know instantly whether it was incidental or a threat. Your heart is beating rapidly and your mind is totally in tune with your surroundings. You can feel our auras reaching out to each other, yet, although we are the only people in this cave, you're uncomfortable."

"It isn't so much that I'm frightened. It's more a sense of anticipation of the unknown because I have no idea of what's coming next," replied Adrian, quietly.

"The object of your instruction is to multiply these things that you are sensing by an infinite scale, touching not only your immediate surroundings but the entire world through all the planes, and then to teach you to synthesize your conclusions to produce something useful. Some of the situations that you'll encounter will be frightening but understand that the only enemies that you'll have to defeat are the demons already living inside your soul. I understand that you were raised to be a nice young man but I also know that, given the choice between fight or flight, your instinct is to stand up for what you believe in and your gift is that you will always see the steps before you...even blindfolded and bound, you will find the path." She paused, "Consider the next few days as your opportunity to take a great voyage that will be making stops on various islands of your mind."

"I had the advantage of knowing that I was a *seer* from the moment I was born. You, on the other hand, wasted the first part of your life, through no fault of your own, but we'll have to go back to the beginning to teach you things you should already know!"

Before Adrian could reply, Orana melted and the cave disappeared. He found himself sitting crossed-legged on a smooth, open plain and he was completely naked.

The young *seer* gazed around a white world sweeping into the horizon, merging into the sky and the source of the bright light radiating from all directions. There were no sounds, no smells, no taste, and nothing to touch. The warm air was not moving and there was nothing that might offer a sense of scale or direction. Even the ground beneath him had no texture. It was simply flat.

Resting his hands on his knees, palms up, he drifted into the meditative state that he learned from Simian. He opened his inner senses, exploring his surroundings, and recognized that he was truly alone in a world that had yet to be created. Perhaps the first lesson was to fashion his surroundings with the things that were most dear, the world as he might design it.

Before he could concentrate on that single thought, his entire life flashed across the white sky like a coil of film spiraling around, each frame a scene, a moment, and it was all happening in reverse. He saw his friends, his fellow *seers*, the animals and their plane, the battle on the island, Ponte's library and the Golden Crystal, the House of the Four Seasons, the inside of the lairs of the Dark Forces and the pulsing red *orb* that had held his spirit, the Wailing Wall and the Basilica in Rome, the Island of the Children and the world under the sea, and all of his challenges and adventures from the first day he arrived on the Morgan's Knot. Farther back, his memories roamed through his home on the bay, the children who attended his school, the sensation of piloting a sailboat, his father's strength, and his mother's warm embrace.

He could see every detail of his bedroom, his favorite toys, his books, and his teddy bear lying on his red bedspread. The salt air blowing in from the bay made the curtains billow like the veils of angels, as his mother used to whisper as she cradled him in the rocking chair, and the morning sun created long feathers of light that crept across the blue carpet on the floor. Suddenly, he was an infant with no cares in the world other than being safe, warm, and well fed.

He opened his eyes and took in the endless white plain, bare to the horizon in every direction, except, in the distance, he could see a small dark lump. He stood and began to walk to it. With nothing against which he might gauge distance, walking across the white plane seemed slow and futile, so he started to trot and then to run as fast as his legs would carry him.

Finally, breathlessly, he approached the object of his fascination, fell to his knees, and realized that it was moving. It was a baby. He knew that face from the pictures his mother kept in a frame by her bed!

Adrian stopped and stared at the tiny child lying on his back, smiling, and gurgling with baby sounds. The infant sat up and then stood, as it matured into a toddler wandering around in circles, flapping his arms like a bird's wings, singing a lullaby that he heard his mother sing, and continuing to grow.

Within minutes, the child became a mirror image of Adrian and he found himself staring into his own blue eyes with curiosity and wonder. His other self giggled, as he continued to develop into a young man with long blond hair that slowly turned gray. Tiny lines formed around his eyes and mouth but his body looked strong and firm.

He noticed the scars on his right leg, as the other Adrian slowly became an old man who stooped slightly and moved with some difficulty, favoring his injured limb. A mane of white hair grew down his back and a long beard appeared on his wrinkled face. His blue eyes still sparkled but they looked tired, sad, and wise.

"Am I you?" inquired Adrian.

The old man looked at the young boy with a glare that hinted at his impatience with the question, "You already know the answer. I am you as you are me."

Adrian smiled, "So, we live to be old?"

The old *seer* grunted, "Growing old is not what it's cracked up to be!" He brushed back his hair to reveal scars on his forehead and behind his ear, turned his back to expose more, and lifted battered arms to bare numerous wounds on either side of his chest. "We have paid dearly for the privilege!"

"I would assume that my battles are not finished."

"You've only survived the initiation!"

"Zepallo?" asked the young *seer*.

"And others…as you will learn, the Dark Forces are layered like an onion, as deep as the sea, and more sinister and evil than you might ever imagine. Their tentacles reach into places that will truly astonish you. You'll learn the necessary lessons at Orana's hand but they're merely preparation for all the challenges we face in the future. Even she can't teach you everything that you'll need to know. A lot of it will come to you at the moment when you see the real challenge and the true path to understanding the reality behind the commotion. There are no rules that apply to the things we must do and there sure isn't a guide book!"

Adrian paused, "Is there joy in our life?"

The old man smiled sadly, "Life is filled with joy and wonder. It's everywhere and in everything. It's in every child's smile, every animal that you will encounter, every day that ends without a battle, and every calm moment that you enjoy. Looking back on it all, I would say that you should be thankful for every normal day. Days when nothing happens, when you could be bored, when things are confined to everyday routines, those are most precious."

"We all take life for granted. New days arrive with every sunrise. Used-up days disappear and are replaced. We just assume that this pattern will go on forever and we don't pay enough attention to the little things that are the very reason for our struggles. Take the time to enjoy the most simple moments in life. That's what it's all about."

"I notice a great sadness in your eyes," whispered the young *seer*.

"We've paid a heavy price for our beliefs," replied the old man, quietly.

"Was it worth it?"

The old *seer* pressed a crooked finger to his lips for a moment, as he thought about the question, then burst out laughing and it took a while to ripple through his system, "I honestly don't know the answer to your question. We're not finished yet!"

"You know what I mean!"

"I know, I know. I'll tell you this much, we succeed. Whether the price that we've paid for insuring the survival of the Powers was worth it...yes, I guess it was. There's something else that you must know and that is that you should take the time to really know the people you love and show them how you feel. When you get to be my age, they'll all be gone."

The old man made no attempt conceal the sadness in his eyes. Adrian focused on his family, his friends, and all of the people and animals who inhabited his world. He could not imagine outliving all of them, let alone surviving to be this ancient person standing before him.

"How old are you?"

"How old are we?" corrected the older Adrian. "Well, I guess that I'm approaching three-hundred years. We have great-great-great-great-great grandchildren. There are hundreds and I have to confess that I only know a few of them. You'll find two things that inhibit your ability to move about the world. The first is that this body will eventually tire, small wonder after all the punishment we put it through, and the thought of spending time alone becomes more inviting. The second is that we become infamous. Everywhere I go, I'm mobbed by people who want to touch me or to be touched by me. They seem to think that we have some magical power that will save their lives or cure their illnesses or make them rich. We don't."

The young *seer* smiled. He knew the feeling, as he was always unnerved by the notoriety that resulted from his missions. He could not imagine having to deal with it for the rest of a very long life, "We are shy, aren't we?"

The old man snickered, "That's a nice way to put it. Yes, I still don't like being recognized. The things that we've accomplished had nothing to do with chasing fame or fortune. As you already know, we did it because it was the right thing to do. As you have so often said, 'There is no other choice'."

Adrian nodded, "If there was only one thing that you could tell me, one thing that might help me through the hard parts that lie ahead, what would it be?"

The ancient *seer* sat down on the white ground, crossed his legs, and said, "Listen to your heart. It won't lead you astray. Give love but don't expect it in return. True love is found in the act of giving from your soul and you will know great love in your life."

The old face suddenly crinkled into a mischievous grin, "You already have the love of your life. You just haven't realized it yet but you will."

Adrian was stunned. He was certainly attracted to Morgan. She was beautiful and one of the few people that he felt completely comfortable with…and there was Alius, who was more like a sister and a partner than a girlfriend. He thought about all of the girls and young women in his life and really had no idea who he would choose, if that decision had to be made in this moment.

The old man watched the subtle changes in the expressions on Adrian's face, as he worked through the problem, "Don't waste your time on this. You're a bit young to be considering these things. Just know that, throughout your life, the women hold the key to your happiness and your success…and your survival, for that matter. Love them with all your heart and, when the time comes, the answer to this puzzle will become painfully obvious."

"I'm confused. I thought that Orana said I was going to learn all of the things that I missed as a child?" inquired Adrian, sitting to face his older self.

"All the things that you missed are already inside you. They've always been there and you've been smart enough to follow your instincts, your hunches, that feeling in your gut. You had no reason to develop your talents until you reached Morgan's Knot, because our dear mother neglected to inform us of these wonderful gifts, but we always knew there was something different about us, didn't we?" The old man's face crinkled into a knowing smile, "You've done well but it will get harder as you go."

"I think the lesson that you're supposed to learn from our conversation is that all of those powers course through your system but no one has ever given you any instruction about what to do with the talents that you've already discovered, let alone those you have yet to learn. You just need to let your energy flow out into the world around you. It will move like ripples on a pond, flowing out to touch everything and everyone in your field of focus, and those vibrations will return with information that your senses can interpret."

"Our battle with Zepallo is a good example. We knew that he couldn't win before the first blow was struck but you also knew that he would survive."

"So, Zepallo is not truly defeated?"

"No, he will rise again and he'll become more powerful and frightening than in the past. Those, who held him in check, went down in that submarine our friends destroyed. There's no one to keep him from pursuing his dreams of world domination. He is a wild child sowing seeds of destruction without restraint and there will be none, other than you."

"I guess I knew that when he saluted me, after our battle on the island."

"That salute was his way of saying that you will meet again. He showed respect for your powers but rest assured, he is not finished with you. There is more to all of this but I'm afraid that we will have to learn it as time goes by."

Adrian started to protest but the old man smiled and patted him on the knee, "Rules of the game and all that!" He paused, "Now, the reason that we are having this chat at the beginning of your instruction is that you must understand that you, and you alone, are the only sentinel who stands in the way of the Darkness. Certainly, you will have help to win many battles and you'll drive them deeper underground but I'm not sure that we win the war. You'll lead the World to long periods of peace and the people and the animals will recognize you as a savior. Don't let it go to your head. It means nothing. See your triumphs for what they are…momentary pauses in an ongoing campaign. Enjoy those times…and use them to rebuild your strength, to expand your talents, and to be with those you love. After all, they are the reason that we do the things we do. You should also know that each battle will demand more of you than the last. As you grow, learn, and develop your strengths, so do your adversaries."

"So, what's the key?"

"The key is something that Master Chi has already revealed to you, 'If you truly believe in the Power of the Light…if you truly believe in yourself, you'll never be defeated.' That's what makes us different, we really do believe."

"Will that belief be tested?"

The old man burst out laughing, "Of course it will be tested! You've already been tested and you know the feeling we get just before going into battle. Your fear and your doubts will save your life. It is in those moments that you will truly see the course that you must follow, just as you did when you faced Zepallo over the eastern ridge of Morgan's Knot. You knew that he couldn't defeat you and your whole being was focused on that evil smile on his face. Everything else disappeared and, in that instant, you both knew that he could not win."

"That was strange. I wasn't really afraid of what might happen because I already knew the outcome in my heart."

"That's it. You knew and you will always know. All of these other things, that you've learned or will come to understand, are inconsequential. They're just tools that you'll learn to use to your advantage. It is that ability to see through the chaos that sets you apart."

Adrian felt a sense of confidence flush through his body. He sat up straight and faced himself.

"Don't get too full of yourself. There will be many times that you'll doubt your own capacity, your judgments, and your powers...and there will be failures and setbacks. Our depression is debilitating but you'll learn that your escape from that state is accepting the truth...when you truly see, you'll find your focus. There will be times when you'll wish to be just a normal person and that someone else would take on your responsibilities. You already know that you can't be 'normal,' you can only follow your path and do your best...and you will pay dearly, in spite of this knowledge."

The look on the old man's face was sad and, at the same time, strong and determined. Adrian stared into his old blue eyes and felt that strength flowing between them. He wanted details but knew that this conversation was being presented to guide him through the other lessons that he was about to endure.

"It's strange, but I'm not afraid of facing our enemies. I'm more afraid of losing those who mean the most to us."

"That's as it should be and another reason that you will find success. You have to defend those who are special to you and, in the process, you'll free the people of the world from the one thing that they can't escape. Fear."

"Fear?"

"Yes, Fear...with a capital 'F.' Look around at the world that you're living in...not Morgan's Knot...but the real world. What drives everything? Fear! Fear of not having enough or accomplishing enough or not being enough. Fear that someone or some group will come along and take your possessions, your love, or your life. The governments, the religious institutions, and the giant corporations use fear to control, mobilize, and suppress the masses. It is the driving force in this world and you must find a way to put an end to it. Believe me, it is the best thing that we do, although...at the time, we don't realize that our efforts will result in that freedom for everyone else. It just happens."

Adrian was dumbfounded. How could he possibly affect the things that everyone else in the world felt? *That's impossible!*

"I can see that you doubt what I'm saying. Don't. It's a waste of time and energy. Just understand that removing fear is one of the things that we have to accomplish in this battle between Light and Dark. It will not happen because you plan it. It will happen because you'll do what you feel is right and true. It's as simple as that."

"No pressure there!"

"There is no pressure in what I'm telling you. It is simply the truth."

"That's been and will always be the motivation behind the things we do," replied the young *seer*. "Our powers depend on that belief."

"Now you're seeing. Don't get hung up on the eventual outcome or benefits of your efforts. Just do what you must."

"What will you do now?"

The old *seer* paused and reflected on the question, "I don't really know. I'm sure that we are not finished with the things that must be attended to, the times change but evil still lurks just beneath the surface and rears its ugly head when we least expect it. I'll admit that I'm getting a bit tired. I've thought that I might move in with Orana and let some of the youngsters take on a more public role but I'm not sure that she would consent."

"Orana's still alive?"

"Of course she is! We're both taking lessons from her, aren't we?"

Young Adrian was speechless. He stammered, "You're taking lessons from Orana?"

"I guess you inspired me to reach a little further and, I have to say, there are some wonderful things that we never dreamed possible…but, then, you have enough to worry about for the moment!"

The boy stared into the old man's eyes. There was so much there and yet, Adrian felt he was hiding parts of it, important parts, perhaps. "When I get to be you, will I be proud of our accomplishments?"

The old man sat up straight and looked directly into the young *seer's* eyes, "Yes, you will be proud...but you'll also be humbled...happy to have known love, sad to have outlived it...proud of the changes that will happen in the world during our lifetime but nostalgic for the...I don't know, innocence and wonder of first learning about the Powers and the Balance. Maybe that's it, the Balance I mean. Life balances out. There's more good than evil. There's more love than hate. What you put into life is certainly returned many fold but there's always a price to pay for the things that we hold most dear. I'll leave it at that. Let's try to leave the world in balance with itself before we go. Fair enough?"

With a wink, the old *seer* vaporized into a rainbow colored mist drifting across the plane in a dissipating cloud. Adrian was left alone in the white world to contemplate his future, pondering the question, "And how are we going to do that?"

The adventure continues in

Islands of the Mind

Morgan's Knot - A Serial Fantasy
Episode VI

Adrian embarks on a lonely journey to discover his own truth and his place in preserving the Powers against the threat of Legio Obscurum and worldwide oppression.

Visit: www.morgansknot.com

Eric T. Stiller is the author of the Morgan's Knot Serial Fantasy as well as a new series of adult novels. He is an award-winning commercial photographer, an educator and advocate, and a Master Gardener. Visit: www.rickstiller.com for more of his work.

If you enjoyed this story, please give it a five-star review on my Amazon sales page and like my 'Eric T Stiller – Author' page on Facebook.